I0538044

Ronald Oleander, Ronnie to his friends, has been looking forward to this road trip for months, ever since he'd aced the test for his motorcycle license. With the wind on his face, he follows Noah and Adam—his older brother and his brother's mate—through winding back roads. Their destination is a small town in Wisconsin where they're meeting up with Adam's old biker gang. Ronnie has been warned the place is homophobic and never to go anywhere alone. Except, when he arrives, the first thing he notices is an enticing smell. Ronnie wanders around the back of the diner to investigate and finds a pair of humans pounding on a smaller guy. Breaking up the fight, he sends the jerks packing. When he focuses on the beaten man, he discovers he's the source of the smell—and is also not only a shifter, but his mate—Hector Ramirez, an armadillo shifter. At barely twenty-one, Ronnie didn't expect to find the other half of his soul so soon, and he doesn't feel ready. Still, he can't deny his instincts. For better or worse, can Ronnie accept not only a mate but figure out a way to stop the people after him?

ArMaDillo Packin'
Copyright © 2020 Charlie Richards
ISBN: 978-1-4874-2966-9
Cover art by Angela Waters

Published by eXtasy Books Inc or
Devine Destinies, an imprint of eXtasy Books Inc

Look for us online at:
www.eXtasybooks.com or www.devinedestinies.com

ArMaDillo Packin'
Kontra's Menagerie: Book Twenty-Eight

By

Charlie Richards

DEDICATION

Being deeply loved by someone gives you strength, while loving someone deeply gives you courage.
~Lao Tzu

CHAPTER ONE

"How's she handlin'?"

Ronald Oleander — Ronnie to his friends — smirked as he flicked his gaze to Adam Kingston's broad back where he drove his *Harley* a few feet in front of him. The white tiger shifter had asked that very question three times so far — twice the previous day and now just then. He knew the man was worried about him, as this was Ronnie's first road trip with him, but come on!

"Just like I told you yesterday," Ronnie replied, doing his best to keep his exasperation out of his voice. "She's handlin' like a dream. After all, you fitted her to my body type."

It was true, too.

Ronnie had met Adam almost eight years before when he'd been thirteen years old. He'd been a scrawny, gangly teen, who'd only learned how to shift into his moose form the prior year. His sister, Heather, had been seventeen. They'd been on the run, and Adam had saved them from wolf shifters.

When his older brother, Noah, had caught up with them, they'd discovered Adam was his brother's mate. At the time, Adam had been part of a shifter biker gang. The group had taken them in, cared for them, and fixed the mess that had been caused by the son of their herd's alpha.

Of course, there was more to it than that, but the gist was that Adam and his people had saved them.

"Just makin' sure nothin' has changed since then," Adam replied through the speaker in Ronnie's helmet, reminding him to focus on the road.

1

A drifting mind of a motorcycle rider could be a dangerous thing.

"I know," Ronnie confirmed, smiling as he enjoyed the wind on his face. "If anything feels even slightly off, you know I'll say something."

"Good." Adam turned his head and peered at Noah, who was driving an equally lovely *Kingpin* next to him. "What about yours, babe?"

Noah looked Adam's way, allowing Ronnie to see his grin. "Perfect as always."

Adam's grunt came through the speaker.

Ronnie sighed happily, relishing the rumble of the *Harley Electra Glide Ultra* between his thighs. The bike had been bigger than what his brother had expected him to pick for his first motorcycle, but over the last few years, he'd grown like a weed and bulked up. He knew it had everything to do with his moose shifter genetics. At twenty-one years old, Ronnie found himself standing at six-foot-three, and neither Noah nor Adam could say if he had stopped growing, yet.

He'd needed something he could keep even if he added another couple of inches.

"Are you comfortable on these windy roads, Ronnie?" Noah asked, glancing over his shoulder at him. "We're not going too fast, are we?"

Ronnie rolled his eyes even as he grinned. "I'm good, bro. Don't worry. I got this."

"It's just, it's your first time out on a road trip with us," Noah continued, expressing his concern. "So if you need to stop and rest, let us know."

"Relax, babe," Adam rumbled, glancing his mate's way. "He's fine. He can handle her."

Ronnie warmed at the praise. "Thanks, Adam."

Noah chuckled. "Naw, babe. Ronnie wouldn't ever be able to handle a *her*."

Adam's deep laughter sounded even over the roar of the engines. "True dat."

Shaking his head, Ronnie joined in the laughter. They were right, after all. When he'd only been thirteen, he'd been confused about his feelings. While the other boys in their herd had been beginning to notice girls, Ronnie hadn't been.

It all became crystal clear when Adam had introduced him to his alpha — Kontra Belikov. The grizzly shifter had been huge with silver-flecked hair and an imposing bearing. Instead of being afraid of the man, he'd found himself enamored with him. While the gang had been in town, Ronnie had followed Kontra around like a puppy dog.

Looking back on that, Ronnie felt a bit of embarrassment. The bear shifter hadn't minded, even though he'd probably scented his arousal a time or two. Of course, the man wasn't interested in him as more than a mentor. Plus, well, Ronnie had been only thirteen at the time, so even if he *hadn't* had a mate, no way would Kontra have touched him.

"Oh, hey," Adam exclaimed, glancing over his shoulder at him. "Did you tell that human guy you were hookin' up with that you were goin' out of town?"

Ronnie felt his cheeks heat as Noah barked, "What? What human guy?"

"Uh —" Ronnie could see Adam's back muscles tighten, even under his leather jacket.

"It was nothin'," Ronnie quickly stated, doing his best to smooth it over. "Just a human guy I was studying the motorcycle test with. And, yeah. I told him I was headed out with you all."

With the way they were roaring down the road on motorcycles, Ronnie mentally crossed his fingers that his brother wouldn't be able to scent the little fib.

"Good," Noah grumbled. "The thought of you doing anything with anyone is —" He stopped and shook his head.

3

Ronnie spotted Adam eyeballing him in his side mirror, so he shrugged.

Adam refocused on the road.

As a young horny shifter, Ronnie wanted to get his rocks off as much as the next man. Unfortunately, after his sister, Heather, had bonded with the alpha of their herd, no one would touch the alpha-mate's younger brother. He'd turned his attention to humans.

Ronnie had always been discreet with his hook-ups. He would find a like-minded guy in the next town over, and they would have a little fun. He made certain he never saw a guy more than a couple of times, since he didn't want to lead anyone on.

Being a shifter, Ronnie knew he had a fated mate out there somewhere. Plus, he was young. No way was he ready to settle down.

One day the prior spring, Ronnie had been running late for his shift at the garage where he worked with Adam. He'd thought the soapy wipe-down would be enough. It hadn't been.

When Ronnie walked into the garage, Adam had just closed the office door where he knew Noah was doing paperwork. The cat shifter had grabbed his arm, stopping his forward momentum. He'd not-so-discreetly sniffed.

Ronnie had felt his face go up in flames.

Fortunately, Adam had chuckled and warned, "Shower next time." He'd patted him on his back as he moved around him. Just when Ronnie had thought that would be it, Adam had turned to face him, walking backward. "And even if it's a guy, make sure to use a condom. Don't want any suspicions, yeah?"

Nodding on instinct, Ronnie had begun to follow him. After all, he needed to get to work.

Adam had spun around, then asked over his shoulder,

"You need me to pick up rubbers or lube for ya?" Then he paused and pivoted, staring at him with his eyebrows furrowed. "I guess I just assumed." Rubbing the back of his neck, Adam lowered his voice. "You *have* had the discussion about safe sex, right? Proper prep and all that?"

Ronnie hadn't thought his face could get any hotter . . . but it had.

"Yeah," Ronnie had muttered. "I'm good."

After a quick nod, Adam had muttered, "Well, you know where I am if you ever need anything." Then the shifter had gotten to work.

They'd never spoken of it again, which was just fine by Ronnie.

The fact that Adam had remembered that he might be leaving someone behind was sort of . . . nice.

They drove for another three days, enjoying the sights and taking detours when they wanted to check something out. At night, they camped and let their animals stretch their legs. Sometimes they stopped and hiked.

Ronnie could imagine himself living this sort of life for decades, and he realized the sacrifice Adam had made for all of them when he'd stayed put for Noah's sake, since he'd been raising him and Heather when they'd met.

All that could change, though. They were to meet up with Adam's old gang that afternoon. Adam had explained that he'd turned his garage over to a fellow moose shifter, and if all went well during Adam's two-month hiatus, the guy would buy the garage, leaving them all free to travel for however long they wanted.

Ronnie was keeping his fingers crossed.

"Now remember," Noah warned, and not for the first time. "This town is full of homophobes, so don't go anywhere alone."

"Got it," Ronnie replied, as he always did. He knew his brother worried. After all, he was more father than brother after all these years. Their parents had died when he was three, and he didn't remember them much. "Where are we meeting them?"

"A place called Mindy Lu's Diner, right on Main Street," Adam told him. "She's a homo-hating bitch, so we won't be eating there. The food probably wouldn't be safe." Glancing at him and Noah, Adam added, "We just like to give 'em shit."

Ronnie laughed.

That is so Adam.

After another few minutes, houses began appearing steadily on either side of the winding road. Side roads disappeared amidst the trees. A *Welcome to Rusty Cave* sign appeared ahead.

"Is there actually a cave around here?" Ronnie asked curiously.

"There is," Adam replied. "And a cave tour. You interested?"

"Hell yeah," Ronnie responded, excitement coursing through him. "That'd be so cool!"

"Language," Noah commented absently.

Adam laughed, and Ronnie snorted.

Noah sighed. "Sorry."

Ronnie grinned. "Naw, bro. It's nice." It was, too. "It means you care."

Glancing over at him, Noah cast a warm, loving smile his way.

I really do have the best brother.

Spotting the diner that they were supposed to meet the others at, Ronnie followed, pulling into the parking lot. He didn't see any other motorcycles. Easing into a spot next to where Adam and Noah were parking, Ronnie rested his bike on the kickstand.

6

When Adam turned off his bike, Noah and Ronnie followed suit.

"I'll call Yuma," Adam told them, pulling off his helmet before grabbing his phone.

Ronnie knew Adam was referring to his good friend and fellow biker, penguin shifter Yuma Belikov.

Taking advantage of the pause, Ronnie removed his own helmet as he swung his leg over his bike. He rested the strap over his handlebar, then scrubbed his fingers through his shaggy hair. Sighing, he enjoyed the scalp massage.

At the same time, Ronnie began walking around his bike, stretching his legs. He made a couple of laps before pausing on the sidewalk. He twisted one way, then another.

Who would have thought that hours on a motorcycle would cause such muscle strain?

No wonder Noah warned me to let them know if I needed to rest. I probably overdid it a little.

Ronnie stretched his arms over his head, flexing his thick biceps as he inhaled deeply. A sweetly musky scent filled his nostrils, making him freeze. It smelled faint but was oh-so-delicious.

Lowering his arms, Ronnie tipped his head back and took another deep breath. His mouth watered, and he hoped it wasn't coming from the diner, since they didn't plan to eat there. Except, the breeze was coming from behind him.

After a quick glance at Noah, who was standing in the cradle of Adam's arms — who was on the phone while petting his brother's chest absently — Ronnie headed in the direction of the intriguing smell.

Ronnie stopped at the edge of the building and inhaled again. The odor had grown stronger, and he felt his blood flow south. His dick plumped, and his pulse sped up.

Huh. Weird.

Hearing the sound of thuds distracted Ronnie from his odd

reaction. He cocked his head as he peered along the alley between buildings. Two men stood over something on the ground, partially hidden by the diner's dumpster.

As Ronnie watched, the nearer guy moved his leg back and kicked at what was on the ground.

Wait. That's a who. What the fuck?

Growling low in his throat, Ronnie felt his moose stir. His animal had turned out damn dominant, so it had been good that he was leaving his herd. He had no desire to challenge his sister's mate.

With his bull bellowing in the back of his mind, Ronnie was in complete agreement. He strode swiftly toward the men, cracking his knuckles as he went.

"Hey!" Ronnie bellowed, anger filling his voice. "What the hell is goin' on?"

The pair snapped their attention to him.

Ronnie could guess at what they saw—a six-foot-three, muscle-bound alpha male—and they would be right. Except, with his biker leathers and closely shorn beard, he looked far older than his twenty-one years. Ronnie had also been told by more than one trick that he would never have been pegged as gay.

The front one lifted his hands in placation. "This don't concern you, man." His lips curled as he cast a hate-filled glance at whoever was on the ground. "This is just a little homo faggot. You know they deserve what they get when they flaunt their deviance."

"Oh, that was definitely the wrong thing to say," Ronnie snarled.

Human or not, Ronnie was going to take a piece of him.

CHAPTER TWO

Hector Ramirez lay curled on the ground, doing his best to protect his head with his arms. The sucker punch from the big blond had sent him careening into the dumpster. He'd bounced off it only to accept a roundhouse to his jaw, and he'd gone down.

It was only because he was a shifter that it hadn't broken.

As much as Hector hated taking a beating, he didn't really want to shoot the homo-hating bastards. For some reason, in this day and age, the one doing the shooting always ended up being on the wrong side of the law. It was nuts.

For that reason alone, Hector kept his small *Bodyguard .380* in his ankle holster instead of drawing it and waving it around. He didn't know if the men would make a play for it, if they knew it was there.

Better to keep it hidden.

Hearing the shout of a third deep voice, Hector tensed. The beating stopped for a second.

Do they have another buddy coming to join them?

Hearing one of his attackers call him a homo faggot that deserved what he got for flaunting his deviant ways, Hector realized they didn't know the stranger.

Hector chanced a glance up from between his arms . . . and just about swallowed his tongue even as a fresh wave of fear crashed over him. The man swiftly approaching was big and broad and wore large black biker boots and leather chaps over dark-blue jeans. His black leather jacket fitted his torso, show-casing wide shoulders. His dark-brown hair hung in messy

9

waves around his beard-covered jaw.

Man in black. So damn sexy.

His eyes, however, drew Hector's attention. They held a thunderous gleam in their dark, dark-brown depths. The anger there seemed almost a physical thing.

Is he going to join them in the beating? I may have to pull my gun after all.

"Oh, that was definitely the wrong thing to say," the stranger stated, his hands clenched into fists.

"What?" the blond asked, clearly confused.

"Wrong." The stranger swung a big fist and slammed it into the blond's stomach. "Thing." When the blond bent over on a gasp, he snapped his knee up and hit him in the face. The guy went to his hands and knees. "To." His big, booted foot slammed into the blond's side, sending him sprawling. "Say."

Then the dark-haired man turned a feral glare at the redhead who'd been helping with the beat-down. "Take him and go." He pointed at his fallen companion. Then he cracked his knuckles. "And if I ever see you around again, I won't be so nice."

The redhead nodded jerkily, his green eyes wide in his suddenly pale face. He did as he'd been told. Helping the blond to his feet, one arm around his waist and the other holding the guy's arm over his own shoulders, he hurried them both away.

As soon as the pair disappeared out of sight, the dark-haired stranger turned his attention on Hector.

Hector couldn't help but cringe, even though the man had helped him.

"Easy, buddy." Lifting his hands, palms out, the man slowly took a knee. "I won't hurt ya." Easing closer, he continued to speak in his deep rumbling voice. "M'name's Ronald. Ronnie to my friends. Where's it hurt, huh?"

Letting out a long sigh, Hector allowed his eyelids to drift shut.

I'm safe . . . for now.

"Hey, now, man," Ronnie murmured. "Open those eyes for me. No sleepin' until we know if you have a concussion."

Hector felt Ronnie's big hands land on him—one on his side, the other on his left arm. They were warm and gentle as he urged Hector to ease out of his protective ball.

Forcing his eyelids back open, Hector offered the stranger a tentative smile. "Thanks," he whispered. "But I'll be okay."

As an armadillo shifter, Hector would heal from all the bumps and bruises within a matter of days. If he could get a hotel room with a nice soaking tub, it would be even sooner. Too bad that was out of the question.

Gotta stay off the grid.

Ronnie leaned closer, sliding his arms around him to help him sit up.

Oh!

That was when Hector smelled it. The dumpster next to him had masked the man's scent. Except, as close as they were now, Ronnie leaning over him and touching him, Hector inhaled his dark, masculine aroma.

"You're a shifter," Hector whispered, freezing in the man's grip. *And not just any shifter.* "You're my mate."

Ronnie stared down at Hector, shock etched across his bearded features.

For a second, Hector thought maybe the man would deny him.

His eyes grew wide, and he even shook his head once. Then a slow smile curved his full lips. He swept his gaze over Hector's form slowly, down, then back up.

Ronnie met Hector's gaze again, and Hector saw a simmering heat darkening their depths almost to black.

"Hello, mate," Ronnie responded huskily.

Before Hector could think up a response, Ronnie slid the hand he'd had on his arm upward. He gripped his nape and lowered his head. Ronnie sealed his lips over Hector's.

Hector gasped in surprise.

Ronnie took advantage. He thrust his tongue into Hector's mouth. Gliding his appendage along Hector's own, he teased and tasted.

Groaning with pleasure, Hector welcomed the invasion. He couldn't remember the last time someone had kissed him with such passion. Plus, this was his mate.

Soft beard hairs slid against his chin as Ronnie tilted their heads, notching their mouths even tighter. He skimmed his tongue along Hector's teeth, exploring.

Hector gripped the sides of Ronnie's jacket, hanging on. His body flushed hot, and he had the almost uncontrollable urge to climb onto the bigger man's lap. He moaned into Ronnie's mouth as his blood flooded his cock.

In response, Ronnie fed him a growl, the sound sexy and low.

When Ronnie's big hand slid under Hector's shirt, Hector sighed, enjoying the warmth of his palm.

Then Ronnie squeezed his ribcage, and pain exploded through Hector's side.

Whimpering, Hector jerked in Ronnie's hold, breaking the kiss.

"Shit, shit," Ronnie hissed, peering down at him as he released his side. "I'm so sorry. I didn't mean to hurt you. I—"

"It's okay," Hector managed to get out, already missing his touch. "It's okay." He tightened his hold on Ronnie's jacket, refusing to allow him to move farther away.

"No, it's not. I—"

"Ronnie!" a new voice called. "What the fuck, man?"

Whipping his head to the left, Ronnie crouched protectively over Hector as a low growl rumbled from him.

"Whoa," the other guy responded. "What's wrong, buddy? We told you not to go anywhere alone."

Ronnie stopped growling and cleared his throat. "Sorry,

Adam. I—" A hint of embarrassment filled his tone as he admitted, "I spotted a fight and had to help."

When Ronnie eased back, the change in position allowed Hector to make out Adam—a fair-haired Caucasian male. The man's green eyes held a hint of concern. He had his head cocked and rested his hands on his hips. Adam also wore leather, although Hector didn't think it looked nearly as good as it did on Ronnie's darker features.

Adam's focus shot to Hector. "Oh. Hey, buddy. You okay?" Closing the distance, he asked, "The guys are here. Eli's with 'em. Want me to get him?"

Ronnie nodded. "Yeah. Thanks, Adam."

Turning, Adam began jogging out of the alley.

Returning his attention to Hector, Ronnie asked, "Can you walk? Or I can carry you." He gently gripped Hector's upper arms, concern flooding his expressive eyes. "Or maybe you should stay here until Eli clears you for movement."

"I can walk," Hector assured. "Nothing's broken."

I would know.

Hector kept that bit to himself.

Except, when he attempted to roll to his knees so he could rise, Ronnie used his hold to keep him still. "I don't know. They were wailin' on ya pretty good." Another low, angry-sounding growl rumbled from him. "Asshole homophobes."

Unable to help himself, Hector smiled in the face of Ronnie's ire. He couldn't remember the last time someone had been upset on his behalf. It felt . . . really nice.

"I'll be fine," Hector assured, rubbing his hand up and down Ronnie's chest, soothing him. He felt powerful muscles beneath the other shifter's torso and wished he could feel them without the layers of fabric in his way.

Hopefully soon.

Ronnie tipped his chin in a quick nod. "Yeah." He gently threaded his fingers through Hector's hair. "Still don't like seein' my mate hurt." His brows furrowed as he muttered,

"Damn. Never thought I'd meet my mate this early in my life."

Hector knew a person couldn't guess a shifter's age just by looking. Once they reached their mid-thirties, they pretty much stopped aging very much. If Ronnie was a human, however, he would have put him at about thirty-five.

Cocking his head, Hector asked, "What do you mean?"

Settling on his ass next to Hector, right there in the dirty alley, Ronnie pulled Hector onto his lap.

Hector thought it should have been awkward, but since he was only five-foot-eight, it wasn't.

"I'm twenty-one," Ronnie told him, continuing to massage his scalp even as he slid his palm down his arm, tracing lightly over the bruising that was already appearing on his forearms. "Hope you like younger men."

Gasping, Hector stared at Ronnie. He searched not only his face, but his scent, for deception. There was none.

"Oh, wow!" Hector grimaced, shaking his head. "I'm sorry. I shouldn't—we shouldn't—I—"

No way did Hector want to bring his troubles to someone so young.

Again, Hector tried to ease away so he could stand.

Ronnie growled and tightened his hold. "Stop that right now," he snapped. Dipping his head, he placed his bearded lips right next to Hector's ear. "I don't know what thoughts just popped into your head, but I ain't lettin' ya go." Ronnie nipped Hector's lobe before giving it a little suckle, drawing a gasp from him, and his dick twitched. "I may not be ready, but you're mine. We'll find our way."

Before Hector could come up with a response, the sound of several booted feet drew his attention to the approaching half a dozen men that were accompanying Adam. Hector tensed. Most of them were big, *really* big.

"Relax, baby," Ronnie urged, rubbing his back soothingly.

"These are the good guys."

Hector had never heard anyone refer to a biker gang as *the good guys*, but if they were part of Ronnie's pack or whatever, he needed to try to have a little faith.

Faith is in short supply.

"Well, this is interesting," a dark-haired man commented, flicking his gaze between them. One side of his mouth lifted in a smirk. "Somethin' ya wanna share, baby bro?"

Ronnie grinned up at the guy. "I found my mate."

Adam barked a surprised laugh as a wide grin dominated his face. "Well, fuck a duck!" he cried, clapping his hands together. "Congrats, dude."

"Thanks." Ronnie pointed at each man in turn, introducing them. "You met Adam. That's my older brother, Noah. They're mates. Then there's Alpha Kontra. Mutegi. Uh, he's an enforcer." Ronnie pointed at the final pair, one extremely tall and slender and the other quite a bit smaller with dark skin similar to Mutegi's. "That's Doctor Eli Raetz," he said, referring to the taller of the two. "And his mate, Sam."

"N-Nice to meet you all," Hector murmured, trying not to feel intimidated. They were all smiling, after all.

Alpha Kontra dipped his chin in a slight nod. "And you . . ." His voice trailed off with a questioning note as he arched one brow.

"Oh, right," Ronnie replied. "What's your name, sweetheart?"

Feeling his face heat, Hector hoped the naturally bronzed skin of his Hispanic heritage hid his blush. "Hector Ramirez."

"Nice to meet you, Hector." Kontra tipped his head to the side as he peered down at him. "If you don't mind me asking, what kind of shifter are you?"

"Armadillo." If it was going to be a problem, Hector figured he'd better find out right away.

"All right," Kontra replied. "Welcome."

"Th-Thank you." Hector looked at Ronnie and whispered,

"What about you?"

Ronnie grinned broadly. "Moose," he told him before pecking a kiss to his lips.

Moose. Wow!

"Okay, then." Eli crouched in front of them. "Let's take a look at you. Shall we?"

Figuring he didn't really have a choice, Hector nodded.

My life just got turned on its head . . . again.

As everyone welcomed him to the gang while Eli looked him over, Hector wondered if they would still feel that way after he told them about the trouble dogging his steps.

I'll need to find out soon.

CHAPTER THREE

As Eli began his cursory exam of Hector's face and arms, Ronnie couldn't seem to let him go. Even though the idea of a mate hadn't even been on his radar — *hell, I'm only twenty-one* — his need to touch the sweet-smelling little man rode him hard. His instincts screamed for him to keep him close.

Discovering him while he'd been getting beaten probably had something to do with it.

Or everything.

Still.

"Okay, Ronnie. I need you to release him now," Eli encouraged. "Let's help him to his feet so I can check out his ribs."

"Nothing's broken," Hector assured.

Eli smiled. "Probably not, but let's just be sure it's no more than bruising, hmm?" The tall, slender python shifter waggled his black eyebrows. "I *am* a doctor, after all."

Once Ronnie had helped Hector to his feet, standing beside him, Noah eased close to him. "You okay, Ronnie?" his brother murmured softly. His expression screamed his concern as he glanced at the slight scabbing already forming on Ronnie's knuckles. "You hurt at all?"

For some reason, Ronnie got the distinct impression that the other man's question held multiple layers to it.

Brothers, after all.

"I'm okay," Ronnie assured, giving Noah a firm smile. "Just a couple of hick human haters. Nothin' I couldn't handle in my sleep."

Noah glanced pointedly at Hector, who was focused on Eli.

17

Then he returned his questioning gaze to Ronnie.

Shrugging, Ronnie didn't know what to say.

Oh, sure I do.

"Hector's my mate." Twisting his lips into a lopsided smile, Ronnie offered, "You know Fate and her timin', right?"

His brother nodded, obviously knowing that better than anyone.

"Well, congrats, man," Adam offered again with a cheeky grin. "I heard through the grapevine that Deacon and his mate, Axel, bonded on their air mattress." With a wink, he added, "They weren't too loud, so maybe you and Hector can top it."

"That will have to wait for a day or two," Eli cut in.

Turning his attention back to the doc, Ronnie growled low in his throat. The man had Hector's shirt pushed up his torso, exposing him from hips to armpits. A wash of jealous possessiveness surged through Ronnie, and he took a step closer.

When had Hector moved so far away from him?

Adam's hand on his upper arm stopped the motion.

Ronnie snapped his attention back to the tiger shifter and growled low in his throat.

Noah's mate rolled his eyes before snapping, "Knock it off. That's the doc. Calm your ass down."

"Take a deep breath, Ronnie," Kontra ordered, his big hand clamping onto his shoulder. "First meetings and injuries set off protective urges like you wouldn't believe. It'll pass." Then the grizzly shifter smiled. "And it's good to see you again."

"Thank you, Alpha," Ronnie replied, forcing a smile before doing as Alpha Kontra ordered. Ronnie took a deep breath. He even closed his eyes for a couple of heartbeats. His heart rate calmed, and when he opened his eyes, he again focused on Hector.

His much smaller mate offered him a weak smile. "I'm fine."

"Not *quite* fine," Eli countered as he lowered Hector's shirt. "They managed to crack a couple of ribs on your lower right side." He shook his head as he rocked back a step. "The bruising will be spectacular for a couple of days, and you'll be plenty sore. Like you said, however, Hector, you'll be fine in a few days."

As Hector nodded, Eli focused on Ronnie. His lips curved into a knowing smirk. Even his dark eyes gleamed with mischief.

"While I know shifter instincts are probably screaming at you to find the nearest bed, wall, or other flat surface and fuck like crazy to complete your mating, I advise waiting at least two days."

Ugh. Hence the mischief.

Waiting would be damn difficult, since Ronnie felt exactly as Eli described. He wanted to spirit Hector away to the closest bit of privacy and strip him naked. Ronnie already knew his mate's compact body fit deliciously against his own, and he tasted better than anything he had ever experienced.

And that ass. I bet feelin' that around my cock will be—

"Focus," Kontra ordered, mirth filling his tone. He squeezed Ronnie's shoulder again before releasing him.

Ronnie realized that at some point while his mind dreamed, Adam had released him, too. He took the couple of steps necessary to close the distance between himself and Hector. Wrapping his arms around his upper body, he gently pulled his mate against him.

Dipping his head, Ronnie nuzzled his beard-covered cheek against Hector's dark-brown hair. "I can control myself," he vowed, even though his already throbbing dick belied his words. "We'll wait. I won't hurt you."

"Of course, there are other ways to offer pleasure," Adam pointed out, his amusement clear as a bell. "Hand-jobs."

"Blowjobs," Eli tossed out.

Sam's voice came out breathy as he murmured, "Prostate

massages."

"And, of course—" Adam began before Noah cut him off.

"Oh, for fuck's sake," Noah grumbled, scowling at Adam. "I do *not* want to think about my baby brother having sex." Crossing his arms over his chest, he huffed a sigh. "But if you need, um . . . instruction . . . uh . . ." Noah's voice trailed off as he stumbled over his words.

Ronnie felt his cheeks heat and prayed his naturally tanned complexion hid it.

"I'll give Ronnie all the instruction he needs." Hector's lightly Spanish-accented voice cut into the conversation, his tone full of possessiveness.

Turning his attention to his mate, Ronnie smiled at him as he admired the man Fate had deemed his. "I'm happy to take all the instruction you wanna give me, sweetheart." He reached out and rested his hand on his hip.

I'll tell him I'm not a virgin later . . . without my brother around.

Hector's deep brown-eyed gaze peered up at him as he dipped his chin in a slight nod.

"Well, then," Kontra's voice cut into the moment. "Welcome to the gang, Hector." He clapped his hands together, then motioned toward the alley's entrance. "Let's get moving. We need to scram before that new asshole sheriff decides to peg us for loitering."

Then, with a shake of his head and a roll of his eyes, Kontra started down the alley.

Everyone followed.

Ronnie used his hold on Hector to urge him to turn and do the same.

"Wait," Hector called even as he followed Ronnie's guidance. "Alpha Kontra, I'm not certain you want to accept me just yet."

A shaft of something icy pierced Ronnie's gut.

Is my mate about to reject me?

Ronnie couldn't help but tighten his hold on Hector. When

his mate flinched and glanced up at him, he felt like an ass and immediately loosened his grip.

"Sorry," Ronnie whispered.

Hector flashed him an understanding smile. Then the man in his arms returned his attention to their alpha, who'd paused and turned to face him. The grizzly shifter had an expectant look on his face.

"What's wrong, Hector?" Kontra asked before shoving his hands in his leather jacket's pockets. "You got a roll around here somewhere? That's what a group of armadillos is called, right?"

A roll? Huh.

Ronnie would never have guessed. He wondered where the alpha had picked that up at.

"Oh, no, Alpha," Hector replied. "Um, I mean yes."

Kontra chuckled, the sound soft and deep. "Well, which is it, Hector?"

After releasing a noise breath, Hector stated, "Yes to roll being the proper term. No to having one around here."

"Then let's get moving," Kontra urged. Then his brows furrowed. "Unless you're afraid of motorcycles?"

Again, Hector shook his head. "It's not that, either, Alpha. I—"

Ronnie could smell the unease rolling off Hector, the scent bitter and acrid. Hoping to offer reassurance to his mate, he stated, "It doesn't matter that you're an armadillo. You know that, right?" He kept his voice low, quiet, uncertain who might be around the corner of the alley. They were next to a restaurant, after all. "Alpha Kontra's gang has plenty of different shifters in it. You saw that already."

Hector's unease didn't dissipate. A tremble even worked through his smaller frame. "It's not that. I—" Again he paused as he swallowed so hard Ronnie saw his Adam's apple bob.

Kontra slowly closed the distance between them. He crooked two fingers and settled them under Hector's chin.

"We can't stay here," he rumbled, his expression intense. "So I need you to tell me now or wait until we're at our campsite."

"There are people after me," Hector blurted out. "And there's a warrant for my arrest in Texas." His cheeks flushed, staining them a lovely red that Ronnie would have enjoyed under any other circumstance. "Regardless of who finds me first, my ex's father's thugs or the cops, you and your people could end up in danger just by association."

Ronnie tensed, but he didn't release Hector.

What the hell could my sexy mate have done to have a warrant out on him? And his ex's father? What the hell?

Kontra's eyes narrowed. "What's the warrant for?" he asked, blunt as ever.

"Drug smuggling for a cartel in Mexico."

Releasing Hector's chin, Kontra crossed his arms over his chest. "Do you smuggle drugs?"

Hector's eyes widened, and he pressed into Ronnie's side, probably instinctively searching for support from his mate.

Ronnie bet the man didn't even realize he was doing it.

"No!"

"Do you have anything to do with drugs?" Kontra pressed.

Shaking his head, Hector stated, "Absolutely not. I had a human friend in high school that ODed. I'd never be a part of that shit."

"Good." Kontra's smile turned predatory. "Because me and my gang have a lot of fun taking out those doing illegal activities." Turning on his heel, he beckoned with one hand as he again began exiting the alley. "We'll discuss the rest at the campsite."

Ronnie once more urged Hector to follow. His mate was stiff at first, tense. He glanced around warily when they exited the alley, his wide-eyed gaze taking in the over a dozen motorcycles and all the men milling around them.

"Holy Maria," Hector muttered.

Smiling a little, Ronnie dipped his head and admitted,

"And that's not even all of them."

Hector peered up at him with his lips parted in shock. "Really?"

Ronnie nodded, guiding him to his own motorcycle. "Really."

Picking up his helmet, Ronnie began placing it on Hector's head.

"Wait," a deep voice called.

Peering to the left, Ronnie spotted Draven heading toward him, a helmet in each hand. He'd met the pale-featured man on several occasions, and he knew Draven was a vampire-warlock. The man was mated with a wolf shifter named Vail.

"This should fit you, Hector," Draven stated, offering Ronnie's mate the helmet in his left hand.

Hector took it. "Th-Thank you."

Draven nodded and walked away, placing the other helmet on his own head.

Ronnie also knew Draven had visions.

Which is probably why he had an extra helmet on hand.

As Ronnie cinched his chin strap, he watched Hector do the same.

And why we were told to meet here instead of at the gang's campsite. So I could meet Hector.

After Ronnie swung his leg over his bike, he used his heel to push down the passenger footholds. "Come on, Hector." He offered his mate his hand. When Hector hesitated, a thought occurred to Ronnie. "Do you have stuff somewhere we need to run and get?"

Even as Hector admitted, "A bag tucked in the woods at the edge of town," he continued to hesitate.

"We need to leave, sweetheart," Ronnie encouraged, noticing the black and white cop car slowing down nearby. "The alpha said the new sheriff is hassling them."

Absently, Ronnie wondered what happened to the old sheriff.

A story for another time.

Finally, Hector took his arm and used the hold to swing on his bike behind him. "Why would he accept me when I told him my presence could put his people in danger?"

Ronnie glanced over his shoulder as he brought his bike roaring to life. "Because you're my mate," he replied simply, then followed the others out of the parking lot.

CHAPTER FOUR

Hector's head spun.

That was it? Two questions and the alpha accepted him?

His mind reeled.

He knew his past alpha wouldn't have acted that way. Of course, his old alpha had ordered his parents to kick him out of the roll for being gay. His parents hadn't objected.

Good thing his sister, Maria, had hurried and packed his important belongings for him.

Hector still talked to her. Well, he had until the unfortunate incident with Dave. He still couldn't believe he hadn't made the connection that Dave was actually David Earnest Wiltmeyer the Third.

Seeing as they had never gone to Dave's house, Hector tried to cut himself some slack.

"Where's your bag?"

Hearing Ronnie's deep voice through the speaker in his helmet, Hector focused on where they were. He pointed back the way they'd come. "I'm sorry, Ronnie. It's the other way."

"It's fine," Ronnie replied with a chuckle. He slowed his motorcycle. "Guys, I gotta fetch Hector's shit. Where's the campsite?"

Kontra's voice sounded next. "Payson and Sam, go with them."

"You got it, boss," replied a guy on a bullet bike as he did a fast, fishtailing U-turn. "Where we goin'?"

As Ronnie turned around — much more carefully — Hector indicated where he'd left his backpack. He expected the doc

25

to turn around, too, since his mate, Sam, was behind him on his motorcycle. Instead, they were joined by a broad-shouldered guy on a *Harley*.

Perhaps scenting his confusion, Ronnie reached back and patted his thigh. "That's Sam Abbott, the beta."

"Two Sams," Hector mused absently. "How —"

"You'll meet everyone eventually," the big man named Sam told him through their comms. "And to answer the unfinished question, Kontra would never tell Eli's mate to go anywhere without Eli before clearing it with him first."

"Huh." Hector glanced from Ronnie's broad back to the other two guys that were joining them to get his stuff. "Alpha Kontra would ask . . . permission from Eli?"

"He always asks mate's permission before separating them," the guy on the bullet bike told him. He cackled a little before adding, "Otherwise, we'll be distracted, wonderin' where our other half went."

Hector nodded even as he realized his past alpha never asked anyone for permission to do . . . anything.

"That's . . . different," Hector muttered.

When Hector heard the bullet-bike guy laugh again before saying, "We're all a little different here."

"Speak for yourself, Payson," Sam commented. "You're in a class of crazy all your own."

"Land likes my crazy," Payson countered.

Ronnie turned his head enough so Hector could see him wink. His big mate's broad grin and squeeze to his thigh told him that their bantering was normal.

With a smile toying at his lips, Hector listened to their exchanges.

I hope I don't bring trouble to these guys.

Fifteen minutes later, Ronnie followed the other shifters' bikes into a campground. He discovered who Land was as soon as Payson stopped his bike with one foot on the ground.

His arms were immediately full of a cute little twink of a human, who ripped off Payson's helmet.

Immediately, the pair went after each other with lips and tongue.

Hector felt his cheeks heat. Sam and a few others chuckled. Even Ronnie snorted.

"They still go at it like that, huh?" Ronnie commented as he eased the motorcycle onto the kick-stand, revealing that he'd seen that kind of greeting before.

"Yep," Sam replied as he swung off his bike. He welcomed a dirty-blond-haired man to his side. "Hi, Ryan. Missed you."

Then Sam had Ryan tucked between his legs while his butt rested on his *Harley*'s seat. They, too, began to make out, although with a bit less ferocity.

"Wow," Hector muttered while pulling off his helmet. "Everyone here is . . ."

"Mated, yeah," Ronnie confirmed. "To men." He held up his left arm. "Need a hand getting off?"

"Later." The word slipped out before Hector could think better of it. "I mean, um, sure." Feeling his cheeks heat, again, he struggled to meet Ronnie's gaze. "Thanks."

Hector grabbed Ronnie's hand and swung off the motorcycle, only wincing a little as pain tore through his right side.

When Hector uncurled his fingers from Ronnie's, his mate didn't let him go. His dark-brown eyes were filled with a heated gleam. He licked his lips, and his nostrils flared.

"I like the sound of later," Ronnie rumbled as his focus slipped to Hector's lips, then back to his eyes. "But I need a little somethin' now, too." Showing off his flexibility, Ronnie swung his long leg over the front of his motorcycle. "Come here, sweetheart."

Ronnie tugged lightly, and Hector didn't fight him. In the next instant, he found himself and Ronnie in a similar position as Sam and Ryan. Resting his butt on his motorcycle seat and spreading his legs, Ronnie tugged him between his thighs while wrapping his other arm loosely around his waist.

After releasing Hector's hand, Ronnie slid that one up and cradled his nape. He used his thumb under his chin to tip his head back. Then Ronnie's head came down.

As soon as Ronnie sealed his lips over his own, Hector sighed, parting his lips just a little. His mate took advantage. He swept his tongue inside.

While their last kiss had been all heat and possessive fire, Ronnie kept this one softer, gentler. He teased at Hector's tongue with his own. His fingers gently massaged his nape. Even Ronnie's right hand on Hector's left side remained loose and gentle.

Hector felt consumed with a deep, sweet ache. His brain began to shut down. He pushed closer to the much younger and larger man.

As soon as Hector's groin slotted again Ronnie's, he felt the hard ridge of the other shifter's erection. He groaned into his mate's mouth. The exquisite pressure caused fire to coil in his balls.

With a groan of his own, Ronnie separated their mouths. "Oh, fuck, Hector," he rasped. "Gotta stop." Pressing his temple to Hector's, he muttered, "Gonna make me blow in my jeans."

Hector moaned again as he trembled in Ronnie's hold. "Ever done that before?" he managed to ask, trying to get a handle on himself. "Wait," Hector countered with a growl. "I don't wanna think about you with someone else."

Ronnie turned his head and nibbled along Hector's jaw until he reached his ear. "No matter what my brother inferred, I'm not a virgin, Hector." Licking his way along the outer shell of Hector's ear, he huskily added, "When the time comes, I'll take good care of you, but no. I've never come in my jeans." Then Ronnie lifted his head, revealing his rakish smile and glimmering dark eyes. "And I don't want our first time together out where anyone can see." Rubbing his thumb along Hector's jawline, he narrowed his eyes. "Call me a possessive asshole, but your orgasms are all mine."

A warmth fluttered through Hector's chest. "I'm okay with that."

"Good."

"Hey, lovebirds!" Payson called. "Chow's on." Then he waggled his eyebrows as he grabbed his package. "Unless you're gonna get it on. Me and Land don't mind a show."

Hector bit back a snarl, but Ronnie's growl filled the area.

Payson cackled, flipped them the bird, then headed toward a campfire.

Ronnie rolled his eyes before focusing a wry grin on Hector. "Payson's an acquired taste, so I've been told." Then he urged Hector a step backward.

"You don't know him well?" Hector asked curiously, confused by Ronnie's word choice.

Wrapping his arm around Hector's waist, as natural as could be, Ronnie shook his head. "Naw, I met these guys about eight years ago when they were passing through my herd's neck of the woods in Oregon." Guiding Hector toward a different campfire—one where Noah and Adam already stood—Ronnie explained, "Adam bonded with my brother, so they stayed there to finish raisin' me and my sister. Us bein' here is our new start with travelin' with Alpha Kontra again." With a wink, Ronnie purred, "And I sure am glad I came."

"Me, too," Hector whispered, feeling even more confused.

"What is it?" Ronnie asked, arching one brow. "I can scent your confusion."

Hector sorted his thoughts a little, then asked, "If you're just now joining up with Alpha Kontra's gang, why would he take a fugitive in, too?"

Ronnie shrugged the shoulder opposite of the arm he held

him with. "You're my mate. Just because I didn't ride with him until now, Adam did . . . for like"—Ronnie squinted his eyes for a few seconds—"I dunno. Decades."

Still unable to make the connection, Hector opened his mouth to ask . . . something.

Adam must have overheard, and he beat him to the answer. "I'm family," he stated, tapping his chest. He pointed at Noah, who was pulling sizzling, delicious-smelling slabs of ribs off the fire. "Noah is my mate, therefore . . . family." With a wide grin, Adam pointed at Ronnie. "Younger brother, so family, and you're his mate, so family."

"It can't really be as simple as that," Hector claimed without thinking.

"Sure it can," Kontra countered from behind him, announcing his presence. "Allow me to introduce you to Tim, my mate."

Hector held out his hand to the alpha-mate—a slender, sandy-brown-haired male. "Nice to meet you."

Tim reached out and took his hand while returning the perfunctory greeting. "Nice to meet you . . ." His eyes glazed a second, and he tipped his head to the side.

Confusion seems to be a recurring thing with me while around these guys.

Feeling Tim's hand still in his own, Hector began to unwind his fingers. He was touching the alpha-mate, after all. He didn't want to piss off the bear shifter by being too friendly with his mate.

"Don't move," Kontra ordered, which only compounded Hector's confusion. "Give it a sec."

Tim's hazel eyes blinked once, twice, before the glazedness cleared from them. Releasing Hector, he turned to Kontra, "We need to go to Texas."

Hector felt the blood drain from his cheeks. Pressing harder into Ronnie's side, he glanced between them. He wondered if the other shoe was dropping and these guys were going to turn him in.

"Easy, Hector," Ronnie crooned into his ear. "You're okay. You're safe, my mate."

Spots danced across Hector's vision, and he pushed against Ronnie's chest.

When had his mate wrapped his second arm around him?

"Not safe," Hector countered.

Is that really a whimper in my voice?

"Tuck his nose against the crook of your neck," a deep voice ordered.

Then Hector felt himself being moved. He struggled as his body was lifted into the air. A second later, he felt something solid under his butt.

A big hand insistently pressed Hector's face into something.

"Breathe, Hector."

Hector recognized Ronnie, but he couldn't seem to make his lungs work.

His mate's broad hand rubbed up and down his spine.

"Come on, sweetheart," Ronnie encouraged. "Breathe for me." Feeling the wide torso he was pressed against expand, then retract, Hector heard Ronnie continue, "With me this time. Deep breath in."

Finally, Hector managed to regain control of his lungs—at least, a little bit. He managed to suck in a shallow breath.

"Hold it, Hector. Count of three," Ronnie urged.

His lungs felt on fire.

"Good. Let it out."

Hector obeyed Ronnie's command.

"Once more."

For the next he didn't know how long, Hector focused on Ronnie's deep crooning voice as he ordered him to take one breath after another. The dizziness slowly cleared from his brain. Soon after that, his mate's delicious scent registered.

Sighing deeply, Hector flicked out his tongue. The flavor of the flesh his face was pressed against exploded across his tongue. Wanting more, he did it again.

Ronnie hummed deeply. "Glad you're back with us, sweetheart."

Hector felt a kiss pressed to his temple, and he relished the feel of Ronnie's facial hair. He'd never been attracted to someone with a beard or whatever before, but damn, did Ronnie's do it for him. His blood heated in his veins, and he snuggled closer as his shaft lengthened in his jeans.

"Gods, your scent is amazingly distracting," Ronnie grumbled huskily. "But I do gotta know what set ya off, Hector. Why the panic attack?"

Tensing, all Hector's arousal fled. He pried open his eyes and glanced around.

Ronnie was sitting in a large folding camp chair, holding Hector on his lap. Noah and Adam stood nearby, as did Eli and Sam. One of them had probably been coaching Ronnie through helping Hector out of his panic attack.

So embarrassing.

Except, Hector dismissed it in favor of pinning a glare on Tim. "You're gonna turn me in, aren't you?"

CHAPTER FIVE

Ronnie bit back a growl just at hearing the idea. Aggression wouldn't help.

Plus, Ronnie knew it wasn't true.

"No one said that," Ronnie told his mate, hoping to continue soothing him. He cradled his jaw and forced his attention back to himself. "No way you're being turned over to the cops for a crime you didn't do."

Ronnie figured he really needed more information about that, too.

"No, Hector, my mate did not make the suggestion to go to Texas to turn you in," Kontra stated from where he stood with his arm around a clearly upset Tim. "That's not what he meant at all."

"Then what?" Hector asked slowly, his eyes filled with fear.

"Food, beer, and explanations," Adam cut in. "Rib night!"

After a quick nod from Kontra, Adam and Noah began prepping plates for everyone. Eli and Sam wandered away after assuring Hector that if he needed anything, to just holler. Beta Sam, Mutegi, and Payson—plus their mates—joined them around the fire.

Kontra introduced their mates—Ryan, Ben, and Land, respectively.

As loath as Ronnie was to do it, he still eased Hector into his own chair. He just happened to keep it as close as possible without them overlapping. After all, they needed the cup holders for their napkins, utensils, and beer bottles.

33

"Okay, then," Kontra began after swallowing a mouthful of rib meat. "First off, Tim has visions. He's part warlock, just like Draven."

Hector gaped, almost dropping the rib bone he held in his hands. After scrambling and securing his food, he whispered, "Warlock?"

Since Kontra was taking a gulp of his beer, Tim answered, "Yeah. Magick and shit. My mother was a witch, and my dad is a shifter. I can't shift because of the magick in me, but I get visions and can do plenty of other stuff." He leaned forward and pinned an earnest gaze on Hector. "I really didn't mean for you to think I was suggesting that we turn you over. I just had a vision that we had to be somewhere near Lubbock."

"I had an apartment in Lubbock," Hector told them hesitantly. "My apartment where the drug raid was. It's how I ended up a wanted man."

Mutegi cocked his head. "Will you tell us what happened from the beginning?" His black eyes appeared almost fathomless in the crackling light of the setting sun. "Why did you have an apartment at all? Where is your roll?"

Hector's shoulders drooped, and he dropped the rib bone onto his plate.

Not liking that response, at all, Ronnie reached over and squeezed his thigh. "Hey. Only if you want to."

"If your gang is going to help me, then they need to know what they're getting into," Hector whispered in reply. His expression was twisted in a sad expression of grief. "They need to know before we go to Texas."

In all honesty, Ronnie wasn't certain he wanted to head to Texas with Hector. He figured it would be a better idea to return to Oregon, to his herd. They could build a self-sustaining home and live off the grid on the fringe of his herd.

Except, as Ronnie peered into Hector's deep brown eyes, he knew that wasn't what his mate wanted. His armadillo wanted a clean name. Ronnie couldn't say he blamed him.

Ronnie dipped his chin in a slight nod. "Okay." Grabbing Hector's wrist, he brought his barbeque-sauce-covered fingers to his lips. After kissing one, he murmured, "Anything for you."

Then Ronnie sucked Hector's index finger into his mouth and swirled his tongue around it, cleaning the tasty goodness from his mate's equally yummy digit.

"Save that for later, huh?" Kontra encouraged, amusement lacing his tone.

At the same time, Noah muttered, "Oh, gods! I don't need to see that."

Ronnie felt a rib bone smack his neck. Releasing Hector's finger, he chuckled. He heard Hector's snicker and knew his plan had succeeded.

I put my mate at ease.

With a wink, Ronnie pointed at Hector's plate. "Remember to eat between words." He grabbed a rib and took a big bite. Around his mouthful of meat, he obscenely stated, "No one 'ere is gonna give ya shit about talkin' with yar mouth full."

"They may not understand you, however." That teasing comment came from Ryan, who smirked and shook his head.

Ronnie just shrugged.

Still, Hector started talking, and his scent confirmed his relief, so Ronnie didn't care.

"I was kicked out of my roll for being gay about fourteen months ago," Hector told them all bluntly. He picked up a rib and stared at it before adding, "I figure that's how most of you ended up in a gang, right? Being kicked out and shit?"

"Indeed," Kontra assured with a head nod. "While times are changing, and we're sorry that happened to you, it does still happen."

Hector bobbed his head as he chewed his bite of meat. After swallowing, he explained, "Maria, she's my sister, she didn't care. She managed to get my stuff and the money I had hidden under my floorboard, and she got it to me." His smile appeared a little vacant and soft. "We'd sneak phone calls almost weekly, but I haven't talked to her for over a month. I'm sure she's worried."

Ronnie needed to touch, to reassure, so he rested his palm on Hector's spine and rubbed up and down his back. "I'm sure Lamar can get in touch with her. He's great with a computer."

Flashing a happy smile his way, Hector murmured, "Thank you. That'd be nice." He took a swallow of beer, then returned to his story. "I found an ad for a guy looking for a roommate. I already had a job working part-time at a local deli, so I still had an income. After no longer needing to give half my income to my roll, affording my half of rent was easy." Hector cleared his throat before sharing, "No one in my roll ever came to check on me in all the time I worked and still continued to work there, and it was only forty-five minutes from our roll's land."

A wave of irritation at the injustice of his mate's roll's alpha washed through Ronnie, but he bit back any comment.

I guess I got damn lucky with my herd.

Being gay there wasn't an issue.

Hector took a moment to take a bite, chew, swallow, then repeat. His eyebrows were furrowed, and he appeared to be trying to gather his thoughts. After a quick glance Ronnie's way, he heaved a sigh.

"I found a gay club in the closest large town and decided to give it a try." Hector's smile appeared pained as he met Ronnie's gaze. "Please don't be angry about anything I say next. I hadn't met you."

Ronnie understood what Hector was telling him. Nodding, he murmured, "I don't have any room to talk. We've both had past relationships." Giving his mate his best understanding smile, Ronnie assured, "The future is ours. The past is just that. Something we'll overcome."

Heaving a relieved-sounding sigh, Hector nodded. Then he glanced around at the others. "I hooked up and had fun for several months before I met Dave. He seemed to be into me, and even though he was human and not my mate, I was horny, and he made himself available." Grimacing, Hector shook his head. "I should have known something was off when he would only meet me at my apartment, and only if my roommate wasn't home, or at a hotel."

"Many of us have gone through that phase," Adam assured with a roll of his shoulder.

Several other men nodded, appearing commiserating.

Hell, Ronnie knew all about it, too, and he was only twenty-one.

"So, two things sorta happened at once," Hector admitted, grabbing his beer and downing the rest of it. After heaving a sigh, he admitted, "First, Dave's dad and some guy who appeared to be hired muscle appeared at our hotel room one night. Dave is actually David Earnest Wiltmeyer the Third, the son of a very wealthy politician in the area." Scoffing, Hector grumbled, "Evidently, he didn't know his son was gay, and I didn't know Dave was deep in the closet. Dave claimed I roofied him, and it wasn't what it seemed. When Dave's father sicced his hired muscle on me, I used my strength to shove past him and flee." Hector sneered at the fire as he added, "Good thing I'd put jeans on before answering the door, or a few people would have gotten a show." After glancing at Ronnie—who gave him a warm smile to show he wasn't upset—Hector turned his attention to Kontra. "Those are the guys after me. They wanna take me back to beat the shit outta me and teach me a lesson, even though I didn't do anything to Dave that he didn't want. It was consensual."

"I believe you," Kontra immediately replied. His lips were pinched in a firm line. "Sadly, the closet can be a dark place for many people who can't seem to find a way to come to grips with themselves."

Once again, there were several grunts of confirmation, as well as a couple of nods.

Ronnie realized that these much older shifters hadn't had the support system that he'd had. He felt for them—really. Then he briefly wondered if he would have had the support of his family and herd if Adam hadn't come into their lives eight years before.

There was a disturbing thought.

Hector's voice returned Ronnie's focus back to where it needed to be.

"I got away from them. Even managed to grab my wallet and phone on the way out, since I'd left it on the table near the door." Hector wiped his fingers on a napkin in an absent-looking manner. His gaze appeared a little vacant as he continued to stare into the fire. "I made it home, although the cabbie looked at me funny since I wasn't wearing a shirt." Scoffing, Hector muttered, "Good thing I'd given him the address to a place two blocks over. After discovering who Dave really was, I didn't want it to be easy to trace where I was. Even though Dave had been to my apartment a couple of times, I know he'd never tell, since he supposedly doesn't know me, and I *roofied him*." Hector made air quotes. "As I was cutting through backyards and side streets, I began to see blue and red lights in the distance. At first, I didn't think anything of it." A second later, Hector's voice took on a strangled tone. "Then I saw Ethan talking with police. He appeared pale, and there was fear etched on his features. I thought maybe there was a fire in our building, and I started hurrying toward him." Grimacing, he admitted, "We'd never been the best of friends, but he'd still been my roommate for over a year."

The color drained from Hector's face as he continued in a harsh whisper, "I was about a hundred yards from him. There was a big SUV between us, so they hadn't spotted me, yet." A shudder worked through him.

Ronnie fought the urge to haul his mate back into his lap. He did grip his hand again, though. Hector tightened the hold, hanging on like it was a lifeline.

"I heard Ethan say he'd never seen the drugs before in his life, that he didn't know I was a dealer." Hector paused, his brows furrowing. "I froze, confused, certain I'd misheard. Then he made a comment about how he'd accepted me as a roommate because he didn't want to be *that* guy. The guy who treated people like a stereotype. I look Mexican. I speak Spanish. Therefore I must be a drug dealer or mule or pusher or whatever."

Hector turned his attention to Ronnie. "Ethan is blond and handsome in a boy-next-door way. No way they'd believe me over him . . . so I ran."

Giving in to his instinct, Ronnie put both their half-finished plates on the ground, then hauled his mate onto his lap.

"You're safe now," he whispered into his mate's hair as he clutched him close.

CHAPTER SIX

Hector thought he should feel like a fool, sitting on Ronnie's lap. He was a grown-ass man, after all. At fifty-seven years old, he had over thirty-five years on the man.

Still, both ages were young for shifters.

Plus, it felt so damn good to curl up in his big, strong mate's arms. Not to mention, he was tired. The long months of being on the run, combined with the beating, the shock of finding his mate, the panic attack, the food and beer . . . it was all too much. His body was preparing to shut down.

Hector wanted to fight it, but he couldn't. His eyelids grew heavy, and he settled comfortably on Ronnie's lap.

Vaguely, Hector heard Ronnie's brother tell him where their tents were. Then he felt his mate's arms tighten around him, jostling, and eventually, something surprisingly cushy and comfortable beneath him.

Even as Hector tried to rouse, Ronnie's deep voice crooned into his ear. "Just rest. I'll make you comfortable, my mate. Rest and heal."

Because he didn't really have a choice—his body was demanding it—he obeyed.

Hector slowly swam to wakefulness. Feeling a heavy arm draped around his upper torso and a big body spooned up behind him, he sighed happily. It seemed so unreal that his boyfriend had finally decided to stay the night.

A second later, reality set in, and he froze.

I don't have a boyfriend.

"Easy, my mate," a deep voice rumbled gruffly behind him. "Just relax."

Ronnie.

I don't have a boyfriend, but I do have a mate.

That thought brought a smile to Hector's lips.

I found my mate.

Giddiness burst through him, and he cuddled back into the large body behind him.

A soft kiss pressed against the nape of his neck. "Mmm, I do like that response." Ronnie nuzzled his face along the back of Hector's shoulder as he began rubbing his palm over his torso. "How are you feeling this morning?"

Hector recalled the painful beating he'd endured, so he took a few seconds to assess his body. "Good," he decided on. "Not as sore as I thought I'd be."

"Glad to hear it." Ronnie began pressing light kisses down his neck, starting with the skin behind his ear. "I know an air mattress isn't the most comfortable thing to rest and heal on."

"Better than the ground," Hector muttered, tipping his head forward to offer his mate more room.

Ronnie grunted while taking Hector up on his invitation. For a few seconds, he suckled on the knobs of his spine, sending the most delicious tingles through Hector's entire body. His skin prickled, his flesh goose bumped, and his cock ached, twitching insistently.

Now, if I could just get his hand further south.

Hector gripped Ronnie's wrist and exerted a little pressure, hoping to encourage him.

It seemed to have the opposite effect.

Ronnie stopped kissing him and flexed his arm muscles. "Sweetheart? Can I ask you something?"

Sighing, Hector turned his head a little so he could peer over his shoulder at Ronnie. "Okay."

"Why did you accept that beating?" Ronnie's dark brows

were drawn into a frown. "I found the gun in your ankle holster. Why didn't you pistol whip the assholes and walk away?"

Hector opened his mouth, then closed it again.

Huh.

"Um, it actually didn't occur to me to do that," Hector admitted. "One of them slammed a fist into my kidney, knocking me forward and into the dumpster. Before I could get my bearings, they'd knocked me down." Feeling his cheeks heat with embarrassment, he told his mate, "I'd never been in a fight in my life. Since I didn't want to shoot them, I just curled up instead."

Ronnie accepted that with a nod. "Okay." Then he slotted up behind him again and returned his mouth to Hector's neck. "Gods, you taste incredible." His words came out a bit mumbled with the way he continued to lick, nibble, and suck.

Hector relaxed back against him. He rocked his hips, pleased to find Ronnie's cock hard behind him. The moisture slicking along his lower back and ass cheeks told him his mate leaked like a sieve.

Inhaling deeply, Hector enjoyed the wonderful aroma of their combined arousals flooding the tent. His senses were abuzz with need. He felt as if his skin was on fire, and he needed Ronnie's hands everywhere to soothe it.

"I want you," Hector murmured, grinding against Ronnie's erection. "Please, take me, my mate."

Ronnie groaned behind him. "Doc said a'coupla days."

Hector heard the whine in the big man's words and grinned. His mate wanted him just as badly.

"You won't hurt me," Hector countered. As he spoke, he tugged at Ronnie's wrist again. This time, Ronnie allowed Hector to guide his hand south. "Unless you leave this unattended."

"Oh, fuck," Ronnie breathed into his ear as he wrapped his fingers around Hector's erection. "Gods, your dick feels so nice in my hand."

Hector moaned as Ronnie began to loosely jack him, obviously learning his length and girth. He trembled in Ronnie's hold as his mate touched him for the first time.

The bigger shifter's long fingers easily wrapped all the way around him. He skimmed his fingers down, teased around his ball sack, then glided back up his shaft. At the top, Ronnie rubbed over his sensitive crown while he played with his foreskin.

"Not cut," Ronnie mused in a deep husky voice. "Can't wait to suck on this."

A deep shudder worked through Hector as the image of Ronnie between his legs and suckling on his dick popped into his mind.

"Would you like to feel that, sweetheart?" Ronnie purred into his ear, slowing his hand's movements. "Wanna see your fat dick in my mouth?"

Hector's voice stuck in his throat. His hips bucked, trying to get more stimulation. It didn't work. The man behind him was too big, too strong . . . and Ronnie had moved his hand from his shaft to his hip, forcing him to still. Hector's throbbing dick jerked and twitched.

Gods, why is that so hot?

Ronnie licked along the shell of Hector's ear, then blew a warm breath over his sensitive skin. "Tell me."

"Yes," Hector gasped. "Yes, please."

Just that fast, Ronnie pulled away. He shoved down the sleeping bag as he used his hand on his hip to roll Hector to his back. Immediately, Ronnie moved his grip to Hector's thighs and pushed them wide.

Hector gasped as his hard cock bobbed in the air. Taking in the feral expression on Ronnie's face as he leaned forward, he twisted his fingers into the fabric beneath him. His abdominals quivered upon feeling Ronnie's warm breath blowing on his damp crown.

"So gorgeous," Ronnie rumbled. His gaze was focused on Hector's erection. "And bigger than I thought." Lowering his head further, Ronnie nuzzled Hector's balls. "Perfect mouthfuls."

When Ronnie licked over his nut sack, Hector whined and arched. The need to get closer to that warm, wet tongue flooded him. His thighs trembled, and his dick twitched.

"Gods, you have a pretty groin, Hector," Ronnie muttered as he nosed over his sensitive flesh. "And smell so fucking delicious."

Hector opened his mouth, hoping to say . . . something — encouragement, begging, a demand — but his throat wouldn't work.

"Love that I've rendered you speechless."

Once more, Hector tried to speak. "R-R-Ron."

"I'm here, sweetheart," Ronnie whispered.

Then, blessedly, Ronnie opened his mouth.

Hector barked a cry as his cock was enveloped in wet heat. His mate had told him he wasn't a virgin, and his skill showed. He swallowed Hector's dick all the way to the root.

When Ronnie drew back up, he hummed. Then he paused a second to slide his tongue over his crown. As Ronnie cupped Hector's sack, he did as he'd said earlier. He ever-so-gently suckled on his foreskin.

Getting a blowjob from Ronnie felt as if Hector had stuck his finger in a light socket . . . but in a good way. His body erupted in a fresh wash of goose bumps. He barely took in enough breath as his limbs twitched. Whimpering cries escaped his throat with no hope of them being held back.

When Hector felt his balls pull tight, he didn't even have the wherewithal to warn Ronnie. As he poured his release into his mate's mouth, Ronnie hummed and continued to suck on him. He even petted the inside of Hector's thighs as if attempting to soothe him.

By the time Hector finished shooting, his body felt heavy and replete. Sweat coated his skin, and his head was floating. Black spots danced across his vision.

A low, husky chuckle drew Hector's attention. He had to blink a few times to get his eyes to focus. When he did, he moaned for a whole new reason.

Ronnie remained on his knees between Hector's spread thighs. He gripped his long, thick erection in one hand, jacking himself steadily. With his other hand, he cupped his balls, playing with himself.

All the while, Ronnie stared at Hector's prone form with a hungry gleam in his eyes.

Hector couldn't move, couldn't speak, even to offer to help. All he could do was watch as Ronnie pleasured himself to the sight of him sprawled before him. From the smug satisfaction filling Ronnie's gaze, Hector knew he was damn pleased with what he was seeing.

And gods, the view of Ronnie jacking off is . . . gods!

Ronnie looked stunning in his leathers, but he was a damn Adonis out of them. His wide shoulders looked like they could carry the weight of the world. He had a light coating of brown chest hair covering his defined pectorals, which led to a treasure trail over his eight-pack abdominals. From the amount of dark pubic hair covering his groin, Hector guessed he trimmed. His erection had to be a solid nine inches and was so thick. It was flushed dark with blood, and the head gleamed with the pre-cum dripping from the wide slit.

Can't wait to feel that in me.

"Yesssss," Ronnie hissed, snapping Hector's attention back to his face. His mate's lips were pulled back in a wicked smile, and his dark eyes appeared almost black. "This is all yours, Hector."

That finally triggered Hector's tongue. "You're mine, Ronnie," he claimed roughly. "Only always mine."

With a deep growl, Ronnie arched and burst. He continued

to jack himself while pointing his dick toward Hector's torso. Shot after shot of hot seed splattered all over his chest, abdominals, and groin.

Hector shuddered at the sensation of the fluid splashing across his sweaty skin. His blood fired in his veins once more as he realized Ronnie was marking him. He knew he would be drenched in his mate's scent for days . . . even after washing.

Ronnie groaned as he dropped forward, catching himself on his left hand. Levering over him, he stared into Hector's eyes as he placed his right hand on his chest. Holding Hector's gaze, Ronnie lowered his head.

"You're mine, Hector," Ronnie stated gruffly. His eyes narrowed as he began rubbing his seed into Hector's skin. "I'm pretty damn alpha," he admitted before pecking a surprisingly chaste kiss to his lips. "And since I can't fuck ya the way my moose is burnin' to do, this'll haveta do for today."

Hector wrapped his arms around Ronnie's broad shoulders. He skimmed his hands over his mate's hard muscles, clinging to the boulder-like flesh. Shivering upon feeling Ronnie massaging his cum into his skin, Hector licked his lips.

"Claim me," Hector whispered, tipping his head to the side.

Ronnie's eyes narrowed, and his nostrils flared. His gaze flicked to Hector's neck, and he licked his lips. The desire burned in his eyes as he again met Hector's gaze.

Then a low growl rumbled from him, and Hector watched in fascination as Ronnie's canines extended.

"Fuck, that's hot," Hector mumbled, arching his neck to the side even further. "I wanna feel those babies."

"Mine," Ronnie snarled, then struck.

Hector gasped as a spike of pain erupted in his shoulder. Just as swiftly, it changed, morphed, into the sharpest zings and tingles. They went straight to his balls, and he unloaded a second time, calling his mate's name with his pleasure.

Unable to help himself, Hector turned his head and bit Ronnie right back.

His mate's roar of pleasure echoed in his ears.

Chapter Seven

Ronnie couldn't stop grinning. Even the ribbing his fellow gang-members had given him about the noises coming from their tent couldn't diminish his happiness. It was all in good fun, anyway.

Fortunately, his and Hector's tent was pretty close to the nearby river, so the water drowned out some of the noise. Also, there were currently no other campers in the campground. As much as the stigma against biker gangs could suck, it had worked in their favor that time, giving them free reign of the place, so they could shift mostly in peace.

Seeing Hector's armadillo form had been a hoot. Ronnie had never seen one before.

Sure, Ronnie hadn't totally completed his bond with Hector, but they'd started it. His mate carried his claiming bite on his neck, and he carried Hector's on his. If he were in moose form, he would be prancing.

Instead, they were roaring down the freeway, heading for Texas. The trip would take a couple of days. They weren't in a particular hurry, since Lamar and Yuma needed more time for their hacking exploits. The pair would dig up any information on not only the case the police had against Hector, but also what David Wiltmeyer Junior had going on.

"Restroom break, boss." Payson's voice sounded through the line.

While a number of chuckles sounded through the speakers, Adam barked a laugh while saying, "You sound like a convict asking for permission from a guard."

Payson cackled.

"I saw a sign for a rest stop in twenty-seven miles," Lamar pointed out. "If we take thirty, I can see if I can get a signal for the internet."

"Sounds good," Kontra told everyone. "It's about time for lunch, anyway. We'll take longer."

Within fifteen minutes, the entrance to the rest stop appeared ahead. It was a small one tucked amidst the trees. The building had two stalls, and there was one picnic table set off to the side.

Of course, with them all being men, they could just wander into the trees to piss. After parking, many of the guys did just that, too. Lamar and Land pulled out bottles of hand sanitizer and placed them on the picnic table.

Ronnie wrapped his arm around Hector and guided him away from his motorcycle. "How are you healing, sweetheart?" Never in his wildest dreams had he thought he had a nurturing bone, but as soon as he'd found his mate, one had appeared. "Feeling okay?"

"Just a little stiff," Hector told him with a smirk and an eyebrow waggle.

Chuckling low in his throat, Ronnie swept his gaze over his man. There was indeed a bulge behind his fly. Memories of his mate's flavor filled his mind, and his mouth watered.

Just as Ronnie began guiding Hector toward the trees to partake in a little afternoon delight, Yuma hollered, "Oh my gods! Ronnie. Hector. You're gonna wanna see this!"

Ronnie peered over his shoulder and spotted the penguin shifter sitting at the picnic table. Lamar was next to him, and they both already had their laptops set up. Their mates, as well as several others, were busy unloading food and drink from the saddlebags of the motorcycles. Kontra stood behind the pair, his feet braced hip-distance apart, and his arms were crossed. He smirked at the screen.

That had to be good, right?

"Later," Ronnie promised before pecking Hector's lips.

Hector nodded, an understanding smile curving his delectable mouth.

They made their way to the table, rounding it, so they could see the screens, too.

At first, Ronnie wasn't certain what he was looking at.

Hector figured it out. "Is that my case file?" he asked, pointing at Yuma's screen.

Yuma bobbed his head, nodding. "Yep. Look at this." He pointed to a specific line.

Ethan awaiting trial.

"That's my roommate," Hector stated, even though everyone already knew that. "What's going on? And how the hell did you get that?"

Yuma turned on the bench seat, grinning. "Well, we have this friend who's an expert hacker, and he taught us a few things." He waved his hand dismissively. "Anyway, it took a little time and patience, but I managed to pull the report about the drug bust at your apartment."

"You're brilliant, baby," Hunter stated, bending and pressing his lips to Yuma's.

Sighing happily, Yuma sank into the kiss.

Kontra chuckled, reached around them, and slid the laptop around the side of the table. Scanning the document, he ignored the couple, who didn't appear to plan to come up for air.

"Looks like your roommate was the one doing the drug dealing," Kontra mused. "Never once were your prints located on the packages." He cocked his head. "Huh. One of your roomie's associates rolled on him. Ethan took you in because you look Mexican, and he thought he could use you as a patsy if things ever went sideways." Scowling, Kontra shook his head. "Asshole."

As Kontra pointed to another line on the screen, Ronnie noticed Hunter lift Yuma from the seat and begin carrying him toward the woods. The heavy scent of arousal wafted in his nose as they passed. He spotted Kontra's amused smirk, just for an instant, before he smiled at Hector.

"They're still trying to find you, but now it's no longer a warrant," Kontra told them. "It's a formality to finish closing out the case. Do you want to go there and clear this up? We'll support you either way."

Ronnie rubbed his hand up and down Hector's back as he watched the play of emotions flicker across his face. Massaging the knobs of his man's spine, he did his best to offer support. He knew his touch soothed, too. That was just the way of mates.

Finally, Hector nodded. "I'd like to finish out that last chapter of my life."

"Good choice," Kontra replied. "It sucks to have loose ends."

"Yes, Alpha," Hector murmured, still sounding a little unsure.

Kontra rested his hand on Hector's shoulder and squeezed as Ronnie gripped his nape and massaged. Between the two of them, Hector began to relax. Kontra offered Ronnie a quick nod, then closed the laptop and rounded the table.

"What about you, Lamar?" Kontra asked the peacock shifter. "Any luck?"

While Yuma had taken on the task of figuring out the issue with the police and warrant, Lamar was looking into David Junior and his activities.

Kontra was under the impression that no rich man was squeaky clean.

Ronnie wasn't going to say it, but he thought that assumption was similar to how many people viewed motorcycle gangs. Most were just fine groups of people interested in traveling on their bikes. It was the one-percenters, sort of like serial killers, the bad guys, that gave the rest a bad name.

"Well," Lamar began slowly, frowning at his screen. "I haven't been able to find anything overt, yet, but there's an awful lot of documentation for art and artifacts of the ancient and rare kind." Shaking his head, Lamar muttered, "Even the richest collectors can't really buy this much stuff legally, can they?"

Kontra leaned over the screen. "He's running for the mayoral office this year," he commented, cocking his head. "And, yeah. Definitely a little questionable that he managed to get a statue made out of an elephant tusk brought into the country."

Curious, Ronnie peered at the picture. "The label says it's alabaster."

Shaking his head, Kontra stated, "Nope. I've seen elephant tusks up close and personal. That's not alabaster."

Ronnie sort of wanted to ask Kontra about that, but then Lamar tapped the screen. "And I can guarantee that statue is made of a black rhino horn, not petrified wood."

"Who signed off on these?" Kontra asked, straightening. "Money is definitely greasing hands. I'm sure the good people of Lubbock would want to know if someone running for mayor was smuggling illegal artifacts."

"I'll keep digging," Lamar claimed.

"After you eat, babe," Rueben ordered, pushing the laptop across the table. He placed a paper plate in the newly cleared space. Lamar stared up at his mate, surprise and a hint of annoyance in his gaze. Rueben smirked. "I ain't askin', pretty bird."

Then Rueben plopped down beside Lamar and added more goodies to the table, clearly intending to eat with him.

Ronnie thought the food looked and smelled delicious.

"Come on, sweetheart." He grabbed Hector's hand and twined their fingers. "Let's join them."

"Why are you looking into my ex's father's activities?" Hector asked curiously, but he followed Ronnie readily enough. "What's the point?"

"To gather enough leverage to make certain he leaves you alone. Don't want you having to look over your shoulder for the next twenty years," Kontra told him, joining them at the food. Tim had already made him up a plate, so as he took it, Kontra added with a wink, "Plus, it's fun taking away the power of guys who think they're untouchable and do illegal shit."

Hector's eyes widened as he chuckled. "Thanks."

Kontra grunted, then walked off with Tim, obviously looking for a place to sit on the grass.

After making up their own plates of hoagie sandwiches—roast beef for Hector and turkey for Ronnie—along with grabbing a canister of *Pringles* to share as well as cans of generic soda, they found their own spot of grass near Noah and Adam.

"So, one problem down, huh?" Adam asked after swallowing a bite of pastrami hoagie.

The gang never did anything halfway. There were always plenty of choices.

"So it would seem," Hector confirmed with a relieved-looking smile. "I hope I don't get in trouble for running. Any idea what the penalty is for hiding from the cops even if you're innocent?"

Adam scoffed. "If they try somethin', we'll all say that you were out of town visiting your boyfriend"—he pointed at Ronnie—"and didn't know anythin' about it."

Hector cocked his head. "Then how do I explain me showing up at the precinct?"

"Easy," Noah answered, since Adam had his mouth full—

53

not that it would normally stop the man.

Ronnie happened to know that his brother tried to round off some of Adam's rougher edges.

"You came back after a few weeks away after spotting a random online article about your roommate's arrest," Noah explained, picking up a chip from his and Adam's canister of *Pringles*. "You wanted to make sure all your stuff was secure." Noah popped the chip into his mouth.

Hector's eyebrows were high on his forehead.

Chuckling, Ronnie knocked his shoulder into his lover's. "I think they were discussing this while we were getting food."

"Damn straight," Adam responded.

Just then, Yuma and Hunter appeared with plates of food . . . and wreaking of sex.

Ronnie bit his tongue.

"Hey, guys." Yuma plopped down near Adam, Hunter right next to him, and Yuma beamed at his friend. "It's good to have you back."

Adam snorted. "Thanks, twinkie," he teased. "I can tell how much you missed me."

"Butthead," Yuma grumbled good-naturedly. Then he winked at Hunter before returning his attention to Adam. "My need for my best friend is completely different than my need for my mate, and you know it."

His smile softening, Adam reached over and squeezed Yuma's nape. "I know it." After releasing him, Adam and Noah exchanged loving smiles.

Ronnie sighed.

I want that someday.

Glancing Hector's way, Ronnie saw that his mate had been watching the exchange with an expression of longing, and he knew his lover felt the exact same way.

Reaching over, Ronnie brushed the backs of his fingers along Hector's jaw. When his mate's eyes locked with his own, he smiled. Ronnie hid nothing, and he knew the promise

Hector could see in his expression.

We'll get there.

CHAPTER EIGHT

Hector walked out of the precinct, inhaled deeply, then let his breath out slowly. He had done it. He'd convinced the police that he'd been out of town, and everything with them had been squared away.

Thank the gods.

Now if I can get Dave's father off my back, all will be well.

The squeeze to Hector's hand drew his attention to Ronnie. He smiled at him. His mate had stood by his side every step of the way.

Sure, he's young, but damn is he confident. So very sexy.

As Hector headed to their bikes with Ronnie at his side, he glanced around the area. Lubbock had been his home for over fifty years. Of course, most of that time had been spent living in his roll's territory, so few humans had actually known him.

Hector had still watched the town grow over the decades, though. He'd always thought it was a nice place to live, but he knew that had changed. The man by his side was his future.

And one I'm looking forward to.

When Hector rounded the side of the building, he froze. There, parked behind the spaces holding Ronnie's motorcycle as well as Adam and Noah's—both men had accompanied them—was a large, truck-style limousine. A man in a black suit stood at the driver's side door. Another stood further back at a rear passenger side door. Both wore shades, but it was obvious they were watching Hector's group approach.

"They can't do anything to you," Ronnie murmured encouragingly. "We're in a public parking lot outside the police station."

Hector swallowed hard before nodding once. He managed to get his feet moving again. When Adam moved to his other side, he was in the process of sliding his phone into his jacket pocket. Noah dropped back to walk behind him, and Hector's heart settled a little bit.

These shifters had his back.

Gods. When was the last time that had happened?

Even when Hector had been part of his roll, he'd been a pretty low ranking member. He really didn't have a dominant bone in his body. Hector followed orders and contributed, but that was about it. His parents had several other children, and they were all more dominant, so they doted on them instead.

Don't bother thinking about them.

When they were about five feet from their motorcycles, the guy standing near the rear door opened it.

Immediately, David Junior's voice came from the interior, even if they couldn't see him, yet. "Get in the vehicle, Hector," he ordered. "You don't want your problems to harm others, do you?"

"He's holding the hand of another man, sir," the guard by the door stated.

The distinctive sound of a sneer filled the air. "Perverting another already," he snarled, his tone dripping with disgust. "Bring them both, then."

"None of us are goin' anywhere with you," Ronnie claimed, using his bulk to guide Hector toward the bikes. At the same time, he tugged on Hector's arm and positioned himself between Hector and the limo.

"You're making a big mistake, Hector," David continued, his voice harsh. "Show him, Greg."

The man near the front of the limo, Greg the driver, pulled his jacket away from his body a little and revealed a gun in a shoulder holster. A chill went down Hector's spine. Sweat popped out on his temples. While they *were* shifters, bullets to the brain or heart could still kill them.

"You know what," Adam piped up. For some reason, there was amusement in his tone. "I think maybe we should *all* go." Adam winked at Noah, then slung his arm around his waist. "We're all fags, after all."

"No," David snapped, his voice ringing with authority. He obviously expected to be obeyed. "Just Hector and his *friend*."

Yeah, that was a nice way to say that word.

"Sorry, David," Adam stated with a shrug of his big shoulders. "You get all of us or none of us, and your pal's gun ain't gonna change things," he finished with a snort. "Make your choice."

For a few seconds, Hector thought David was going to order Greg to draw his weapon. A tremble worked down his spine. He almost stepped forward to agree, but Ronnie's hold around his waist tightened, perhaps feeling him sway to take a step or scenting the possibility.

"Fine," David snapped. "Bring them all."

Hector didn't know why Adam would suggest they all go, but over the few days of traveling with him, he'd come to trust the man. He might be brash and bold, but he would never do anything to endanger his family. Having completed his bond with Ronnie the evening before — *gods, I can still feel the delicious stretch to my chute muscles just a little from my mate's amazing cock* — Hector knew that he was Adam's family, too.

Adam led the way with Noah right behind. Hector climbed in with Ronnie on his heels. He spotted David to his right, sitting on the back seat. Adam had moved left and across to another bench seat that faced the middle of the car, with Noah beside him. Ronnie guided Hector to the left as well, to the bench seat that sat opposite Adam's.

In other circumstances, Hector might have taken a few seconds to admire the impressive interior. The cushions were soft, and the carpet plush. He bet the paneling on the walls was real wood.

Unfortunately, having to be so close to his ex's asshole father — eh, not so much.

Sitting next to the glass partition, Hector was as far away from David as he could get. When the guy who'd opened the back door joined them, he settled on the back seat with David. Someone outside — Greg, presumably — closed the door.

Then the other guard drew a pistol and pointed it in their direction.

Of course, he has a gun, too.

Adam still continued to grin . . . as if dealing with guys with guns was a regular occurrence for him.

Seeing as Hector had only known him a few days, maybe it was.

The car began to move.

"All right, buddy," Adam began, slinging his arm around Noah's shoulders. He looked like he didn't have a care in the world. "You seem to want to chat with gay guys, David. What can we help you with?" Waggling his eyebrows, Adam continued in the next instant, "Did you want to talk about your sexuality? Coming out strategies? Sexual position advice?" His grin lit up his pale features, and his green eyes twinkled. He snapped his fingers. "I know. You wanna know safe sex practices, like proper stretching techniques."

The more Adam talked, the redder David's face became. A vein pulsed on his forehead. His eyes narrowed, and his jaw clenched as he ground his teeth. Even his nostrils flared.

Hector wondered if the man would break a tooth.

"Enough!" David roared, making the guard beside him jolt. "Shut up, you disgusting excuse of an abomination."

Good thing the man's finger wasn't actually on the trigger. The guard glanced his boss's way for an instant before returning his focus to Hector and his group. His face appeared a bit red, but he didn't seem nearly as affected as David.

Adam lifted the hand of the arm that wasn't around Noah, his palm up, in a *what did I do* gesture.

Hector just managed to keep from snickering. David's next words caused all mirth to flee.

"Shoot that vile creature," David demanded, pointing at Adam.

The guard's eyebrows shot up. "Uh, sir?"

"Don't question me. Do your damn job." David glared at the guard, clearly expecting to be obeyed.

"Uh, sir." The guard tried again. "My job is to protect you, sir. Not kill someone in cold blood." When David opened his mouth to demand again, the man added, "Besides, it would make a mess in your car that would be almost impossible to clean, and there are cameras around the precinct that probably recorded him getting in here."

Huh. A voice of reason.

David curled his lip, but he seemed to take a deep breath and calm down . . . a little. Turning his attention to Hector, he glared, his voice coming out cold. "You have only a reprieve, Hector, because you are next. Did you really think I'd let you get away with roofying my son?"

"Roofying Dave?" Hector shook his head. Perhaps it was the fact that his mate was sitting beside him that gave him the strength, for he snapped, "I didn't roofie Dave. I've never roofied anyone. I wouldn't even know where to get the shit needed to do that." Pointing at David, Hector continued, "We dated for three weeks, and I get why he wouldn't tell you he's gay. I really do. You're a homophobic bastard of an asshole. No wonder he's so damn deep in the closet. I don't blame him one bit."

Hector realized he didn't either. The run-in with his ex's father hadn't truly been why he'd needed to leave town. As an armadillo shifter, going to jail just hadn't been an option.

Ronnie growled from where he was seated next to him. His hand tightened on Hector's thigh. Meeting his mate's gaze, he found Ronnie scowling at him.

"I really hate listening to you talk about dating other people, Hector," Ronnie admitted gruffly. "Please don't."

"I'm all yours now, Ronnie," Hector assured, placing his own hand over Ronnie's and squeezing tightly. "Nobody else's ever again."

"Ahhh, that's so sweet," Adam murmured, sounding happy in a cheesy way. He nudged Noah and tipped his chin toward Ronnie. "You raised your boy right."

"What the fuck?" David cried, half-rising from his seat. His eyes were nearly bugging out of his skull as he glanced between them all. "Faggots raising kids? Vile!"

David grabbed for the gun in the guard's hand, who appeared shocked by his boss's movement. The gun slipped from his grip, giving David a chance to snag it. He began to lift it, leveling it toward Noah.

Ronnie lifted his right foot and struck out and up.

The report of the weapon rang in Hector's ears as a hole appeared in the roof of the vehicle. The limo swerved, the sound obviously having surprised the driver.

The guard lunged forward, attempting to grab Ronnie. Hector's mate met him head-on, taking them both into the back seat.

Noah swung for the gun in David's hand, but he missed due to the driver righting the vehicle back on the road.

Doubled over from the swerving, having been thrown half out of his seat, Hector spotted his own weapon, still tucked safely in his ankle holster. He popped the catch and drew it. As he brought it up, he realized he didn't think he could ever actually shoot someone.

Except then, Hector remembered Ronnie's words from days before.

As Hector watched Noah grappling awkwardly over the back of Ronnie, who was still on top of the guard, he pushed away from the floor. He vaguely recognized the sound of the partition being lowered, but he ignored it. Instead, Hector lunged for David and slammed the butt of his pistol into his temple.

Even with Hector only using half-strength, David's head snapped backward. In the next instant, he slumped in his seat, the gun falling from his now-limp fingers.

At the same time, Ronnie jerked backward, away from the guard.

Hector saw that he was unconscious, too.

A howl of pain from the front caused Hector to snap his attention that way. Adam was halfway through the open partition.

"Hey, guys," Adam called, his voice sounding a little muffled. "Would one of you maybe wanna help me? This guy's out cold, and I'm drivin' this damn thing."

Noah laughed as he eased forward. "How can I help?"

Ronnie lunged at Hector, wrapping him in a hug.

Sealing his mouth over his, Hector happily opened to him. He reveled in the taste of his mate and the ferocity of his desire. His mate threaded his fingers through Hector's hair and plundered his mouth for several long, beautiful seconds.

When Ronnie broke the kiss and peered down at him, he whispered, "Fuck, Hector. I was so damn worried."

"Me, too," Hector admitted. "But we're safe now. We'll be okay."

Ronnie nodded, then began lowering his head again. He paused, and his eyebrows furrowed. His gaze lowered to Hector's hand, and he realized he still held his gun.

"Uh, sweetheart?" Ronnie began slowly. "Were you packin' in the sheriff's office?"

Feeling his cheeks heat, Hector nodded. "I forgot it was there."

Ronnie laughed, and Hector cut it off with a kiss.

CHAPTER NINE

Thanks to the phone app that Adam had initiated outside the police precinct, many of the gang arrived within ten minutes. As soon as Adam had sent the *need help* text, he'd opened the tracking program. That allowed anyone in the gang to follow his phone's movements.

Kontra had wrangled up a dozen members of the gang, and they'd been in pursuit.

Ronnie had heard tales of how they'd used their animal forms to bring vehicles to a stop—from pick-ups to box trucks. He figured it would have been interesting to see how they managed to stop a stretch-truck limo. They hadn't needed to, however.

Between all of them, they'd taken out their captives. Adam had used his slinky cat flexibility to slither half-way through the partition window. While Adam kept one hand on the wheel—Noah telling him to veer right or left to keep them on the road—Adam had managed to move the unconscious driver's foot off the gas pedal.

Before too long, they'd drifted to a stop.

After piling out of the vehicle, Ronnie hadn't been able to allow Hector too far from him. Well, in truth, he'd kept him wrapped in his arms. Every few seconds, he would peck a kiss to his lips or run his hands up and down his spine.

Just imagining the things that could have happened to his mate made Ronnie want to fuck him through the mattress just to assure himself that they were both alive and well . . . after giving him a thorough bath with his tongue, so he could make certain he didn't have any injuries.

Since that wasn't possible on the side of the road, Ronnie resigned himself to cuddles and kisses only.

Even the roar of the motorcycles didn't wake their sleeping beauties.

Instead, Kontra had ordered Mutegi to drive the limo out of town. Ronnie had been grateful when Lamar had swung off his motorcycle and tossed him the keys. While Lamar had climbed on behind Rueben, Ronnie had led Hector to the peacock shifter's ride.

While Lamar didn't drive a *Harley* — it was a very nice *Goldwing Interstate* — Ronnie easily made himself comfortable with the machine.

Caleb had hopped on behind his mate, Emmett, giving Adam and Noah a set of wheels to share. Tim, who'd been riding with Kontra, had driven Mutegi's motorcycle.

After that, they'd all followed Mutegi and the limo to an old abandoned gas station almost thirty miles north of town.

Mutegi parked the big vehicle and exited it. A group of the guys went through with a hand-held vacuum and sanitizing wipes, cleaning away all traces of their DNA. Finally, the unconscious driver was returned to the front seat, while the other two were kept in the back seat. Even the guards' guns were cleaned and returned to their shoulder holsters.

Kontra motioned to Draven. "Can you alter their memories?"

Draven's pale blue irises bled to red. "What would you like them to be?"

"They were here to meet a port official to bribe him and get their fake paperwork for a new mosaic David wants. The port official was an undercover cop." Kontra grinned evilly. "And in exchange for leniency if David turns himself in, he'll give up every name he has. They need to go straight to the station after they wake up and talk to Detective Vendin. He's the one who cleared Hector's case. He has a good head on his shoulders."

Draven smiled, showing off his vampire fangs. "Of course."

As Draven started toward the vehicle, intending to do the driver first, Kontra clapped his hands once. "Oh." He pointed at the back. "And David is pulling his nomination for mayor."

Chuckling, Draven nodded. Then he leaned into the cab of the vehicle and started his task.

"Just like that?" Hector asked, clearly shocked at how easy it must seem.

Kontra shrugged. "Sometimes the simple way is best." He waved a hand at his people who were hanging out and laughing together. "Although, it didn't start out this easy. My gang has grown and been gifted with many people with extraordinary skills over the last decade." The grizzly shifter's smile held a vast wealth of smug satisfaction. "Fate has smiled on us."

Hector nibbled his bottom lip as he nodded. "Where do we go from here?"

Ronnie sort of thought it sounded like a rhetorical question, but Kontra answered.

"Wherever we want to, Hector." His deep brown eyes held a wealth of kindness as Kontra reached out and touched his shoulder. "Is there somewhere you want to go? Want to see?" Arching one brow, he added, "Anyone you want to visit?"

For a second, Hector opened his mouth, but then he snapped it shut again.

"Tell us," Ronnie urged softly, hugging his mate close. "What thought just rattled through that mind of yours?"

After a deep sigh, Hector admitted, "I would love to see my sister, Maria, again before leaving town."

"Then we'll do it," Kontra immediately replied. "Your roll is near here, right? Just to the west?"

Hector's eyes widened even as he shook his head. "Yeah, I mean, they are, but I was banished. I can't go back there."

Kontra's grin held a definite hint of mischief. "If you were a rogue shifter, that would indeed be the case, but you're not." Looking extremely pleased about whatever he was going to say next, he continued, "When you joined a new pack, that rule changed. You're under my protection now, and since I'm about to travel through another alpha's territory, rules dictate that I stop in and announce myself, my intentions, and how long I intend to stay."

"You plan to stay?" Hector looked confused.

Ronnie felt the same way.

With a wink, Kontra shook his head. "Naw. But that doesn't mean I can't use the rule to my benefit." He pointed to Hector. "And yours. Do you want your sister to know ahead of time, so you can be certain when she'll be around?"

Hector shrugged. "She's always around. Females aren't allowed to leave."

Kontra's eyes narrowed. "Then we'll drop by mid-morning tomorrow," he said on a growl. "Head back to the motel."

Then Kontra spun and grumbled words about controlling asshole alphas as he stalked away.

"Did I do something wrong?" Hector asked tentatively.

Ronnie shook his head. "No, you didn't. Come on." He swung back onto Lamar's bike and helped Hector get on behind him.

"Then what?"

Before firing up the motorcycle, Ronnie told his mate, "Kontra hates it when alphas use their position to force their packs to act a certain way . . . like keeping them prisoner."

Hector nodded slowly, his dark eyes taking on a thoughtful gleam.

Ronnie started them toward the motel. He glanced in his rearview mirror and spotted Adam and Noah trailing him on

Caleb's bike. Smiling, a warm glow settled in his gut.

Yeah, my family is awesome.

Twenty minutes later, Ronnie waved at his brother and Adam and ushered Hector swiftly into his hotel room. As soon as he'd closed and locked the door, he began stripping his mate. In between kisses, Ronnie managed to tear both their shirts over their heads.

Hector's laughter at his antics, and his playfully teased comment, "In a hurry, handsome," caused some of Ronnie's need to ease from him.

Ronnie took a deep breath as he straightened. Peering at Hector, he forced himself to calm down—his actions, anyway. Nothing could ever calm his randy cock for the man before him.

Smiling, Ronnie cradled Hector's jaw. "Just needing to reconnect to the man who holds my heart." Then he began to lower his head.

Hector's gasp made Ronnie pause.

Ronnie noticed Hector's wide eyes and slightly parted lips. The scent of his shock rolled off him in waves. Confused, Ronnie teased his thumb along his mate's lower lip.

"What is it?"

After slipping his tongue out to wet his lips, Hector whispered, "Y-Your heart? I, um, I hold your heart?"

Thinking back over his words, Ronnie realized he had admitted that. "Yes, my mate. You hold my heart," he answered honestly. "I love you, and seeing you in danger makes my palms sweat, my pulse race, and not in a good way." Sliding his arms around Hector, Ronnie rubbed one hand up and down the smooth flesh of his back while dipping the other into the waistband of his jeans, so he could tease his crack and the swell of his ass cheeks. "I much prefer you right here. Safe in my arms."

Hector stared at Ronnie through his lashes. Pleasure

gleamed in his dark, expressive eyes. "Me, too," he whispered. Then he cleared his throat. "Um, I mean, you have my heart, too." Hector pressed against him harder. "I love you, Ronnie."

Groaning, Ronnie dipped his head and pressed a hard kiss to Hector's lips. He broke it for only a heartbeat to growl, "I love you, too, Hector." Then Ronnie couldn't help himself. He needed his mate too much.

"Gods, Hector," Ronnie muttered against his lips.

As he did so, Ronnie picked up his mate and carried him to the bed. Knowing he had to put his lover down, Ronnie finally managed to end his ravenous exploration of his mouth. Seeing the other half of his soul sprawled on the bed, his chest, neck, and face flushed and his eyes heavy-lidded with need, caused Ronnie's dick to flex in his jeans.

"Naked," Hector demanded, breaking the silence. "Now."

Ronnie moaned again, more than on board with that. He swiftly shoved down his pants, only to nearly topple when they got stuck on his boots. Growling in annoyance, he took the necessary steps to unlace and remove the heavy biker boots.

By the time Ronnie straightened, Hector lay naked and waiting in the bed. His compact frame and bronzed skin called for his touches. He wanted to suck up marks everywhere ... especially on the gorgeous cock that Hector was stroking.

"Mine," Ronnie snarled, grabbing the lube off the nightstand. Then he crawled up the bed, slapped Hector's hand away, and swallowed him to the root.

Ronnie moaned just as deeply as Hector. His mate's flavor burst across his tongue—lightly salted pre-cum and delicious male flesh. Nothing had ever tasted better ... except his mate's seed itself.

Soon.

Ronnie poured lube onto his fingers before closing the tube

and tossing it aside. Pressing a finger to Hector's opening, he easily slid one slicked finger into him. His gorgeous lover was still slightly loose from their morning antics, allowing him to slide a second digit easily in beside the first.

Gods, that's so fucking sexy.

Loving that through everything that had happened that day, Hector had still been able to feel him, Ronnie moaned in appreciation. He curved his fingers and teased at his prostate. When a burst of pre-cum hit his tongue, he rumbled deep in his throat with pleasure.

More.

Two fingers quickly became three.

Ronnie listened to Hector's whimpers and whines. Only the grip his second hand had on his mate's hip kept him reasonably still so he could play with his cock and prostate. Judging by Hector's breathy whining of his name, his mate didn't mind one little bit.

Then, finally, with one more hard sucking pull and a vigorous rubbing to his prostate, Ronnie sent Hector soaring over the edge.

Hector cried Ronnie's name as he poured his seed into his mouth.

Greedy for it all, Ronnie continued to suck, although he did manage to lighten his pressure. He wanted his lover kept stimulated, not in pain. The sweet ambrosia of Hector's cum went to Ronnie's head, and he had to grip the base of his prick — *hard* — to keep from coming.

When Hector's dick stopped spurting, Ronnie could wait no longer. He pulled off Hector's cock, using the back of his clean hand to wipe the spittle from his lips. At the same time, Ronnie gently eased his fingers from his mate's chute.

Ronnie knee-walked forward as he gripped his length. He jacked himself twice, then forced himself to let go of his oversensitized length. With a hand slid under Hector's ass cheek, he lifted. He used his other hand to guide his erection where it needed to go.

Then Ronnie thrust.

Hector's body opened easily to him, and Ronnie sank home in one long, bliss-inducing glide.

CHAPTER TEN

Hector groaned with pleasure as Ronnie stretched his channel wide open with his massive rod. Even as he felt his dick give a half-hearted twitch, he knew it wasn't rising again, yet. Shifters might have fantastic sex drives with their partners, but it would take some massive prostate pegging to get there again.

And Ronnie wasn't doing that.

Instead, Hector noticed the trembling in the big man over him, in him. Rubbing his hands up and down his mate's back, worry flooded him. His lover was fully seated inside him, but he wasn't moving but for his body's involuntary twitches.

"Ronnie?" Hector whispered, scraping his nails up his mate's spine in the way he'd found he loved. When that didn't get a response, he dug his fingers into his shoulder blades. "Ron?"

When Ronnie groaned deep in his throat, Hector felt the first dredges of concern begin to fade out the blissful aftershocks of his orgasm.

"Everything okay?"

Ronnie whined a little, then lifted his head. His features were pulled tight, a feral light filling his dark eyes. He even panted harshly through his full, slightly pursed lips.

"Gods, that's a good look on you," Hector whispered, realizing the reason behind Ronnie's stillness. "So fucking sexy."

My mate needs to blow so bad just from sinking into me.

Heady.

"D-Don't wanna c-come, yet," Ronnie muttered through

clenched teeth. "Ugh, not yet."

"Yes, now," Hector countered. With a wicked grin, he clenched his chute muscles.

Ronnie gasped. His eyes widened. Even his body jolted, but he still didn't move.

Narrowing his eyes, Hector lifted his hands to cradle Ronnie's neck. He peered deep into his mate's eyes, and he began to rhythmically milk his lover's erection—squeeze, relax, squeeze, relax.

On the fifth round, Ronnie's eyes widened, and his pupils dilated. He roared out his pleasure. Sliding a hand under Hector's hips, he pulled out his cock, then slammed back into him. Ronnie continued to stare into Hector's eyes as he did it once, twice more.

Hector watched with satisfaction as Ronnie's eyes nearly rolled to the back of his head. His mate stilled on top of him as he embedded his dick deep inside him. The warmth of his lover's seed heated him from the inside out.

Ronnie panted for breath, the noise harsh in the sudden quiet of the motel room. Peeling his eyelids open to half-mast, he focused on Hector. His expression still held a feral gleam.

"Minx," Ronnie grumbled.

Smiling, Hector whispered, "Your minx."

His eyes narrowing, Ronnie roughly replied, "Hell yeah."

Then Ronnie dipped his head and sank his teeth into Hector's neck. He pierced his mating scar. He wrapped his lips around Hector's flesh and sucked . . . hard.

The spike of pain was fleeting, swiftly morphing into ecstasy and tingles and zings of bliss.

Hector cried out Ronnie's name as his body burst, coating them both in his seed.

After several long seconds, Ronnie carefully rolled them. Hector found himself sprawled over his mate's broad chest, and he sighed deeply. He thought about getting up to clean them, but he decided to rest a moment.

Really, there was nowhere else he wanted to be, anyway.

Hector did everything he could to keep from shifting nervously on the back of Ronnie's motorcycle. He couldn't help an occasional adjustment. His nerves were firing through his veins, alternating between a wash of heat and ice.

"Easy, sweetheart," Ronnie rumbled. Turning his head, he didn't use their helmet microphones. Instead, he called over his shoulder, "You okay back there?"

"Nervous," Hector admitted. "Are these rules Kontra talked about common knowledge?"

Ronnie shrugged as he reached up and tapped a button on his comms. "Hey, Alpha Kontra? Are these inter-pack rules common knowledge? Like . . . passed down alpha to alpha? Or what?" After a second, perhaps realizing how that sounded, Ronnie added, "How did you find out about them, if you don't mind my asking?"

Kontra's deep voice came back through the line. "The Shifter Council got a little lax over the last century, but some new members are working hard to fix all that. It used to be common knowledge." He glanced over his shoulder, then slowed his *Harley*. The other gang-members flowed around him until he was riding beside them. "What's on your mind? Worried about our reception?" Winking, Kontra told him, "It's why I left half our pack at the motel. Don't wanna overwhelm your asshole ex-alpha and cause an incident."

As Hector processed that, Kontra added, "Oh, and I actually learned this shit from my father, who was the beta of our grizzly sleuth over a century and a half ago in Germany. He trained me in the way of leadership, since he expected me to follow in his footsteps."

"But you didn't want to?" Hector gaped at the bear. "Then how'd you end up here?"

Kontra laughed. "Long story for another time." He tipped his head to indicate his mate driving a little ahead of him.

Hector guessed it had something to do with Tim.

Okay.

"So what's really your concern?" Kontra pressed.

Figuring keeping secrets from his new gang-members wasn't wise, Hector stated, "I'm just worried Alpha Alberto will attack first instead of listening. He's hella-possessive of his territory."

"How old is he?" Kontra asked. "How long has he been alpha? When did he take over?"

Hector shrugged. "I'm fifty-seven, and he was alpha when I was born. I heard he'd taken over from the previous one six years prior when he won an alpha-challenge." Watching Kontra's broad frame next to them, Hector added, "Was told it was the way of our kind."

"Not all packs are that way," a wolf shifter named Diego cut in. "I was alpha of my pack for over two centuries before stepping down so my son could lead. Some transfers are peaceful."

Feeling his eyebrows shoot up his head, Hector whispered, "Wow. Okay."

A wolf stepped down? Huh.

"Well, anyway," Kontra mused. "If your ex-Alpha Alberto wants to cause trouble, we'll give him trouble, but that's not our goal today."

"Goal?" Hector parroted, cringing at how he sounded.

Kontra glanced his way and nodded once as he gave him a crooked grin. "Yep. Gonna see your sister."

Warmth filled Hector at the idea. He hadn't seen her in so long. "Thanks."

While Kontra remained beside them, Ronnie reached back and squeezed his leg, offering support.

As the scenery became more and more familiar, Hector felt

his nerves drain from him. This place, for better or worse, was his birth home. He had never expected to return, but there he was.

And surrounded by a great group of guys who all have my back.

When they turned down a long, winding path, Hector heard the sound of chittering, even over the rumbles of their machines' engines. He knew it was his roll's warning system. Armadillos would send up a call which would be repeated until it arrived at the alpha's house.

It took less than a minute, while driving along the bumpy dirt road took considerably longer.

By the time the group of eight motorcycles arrived at the central square of Hector's roll, the place was damn near deserted. The only people standing around were Alpha Alberto, Beta Grange, and four other men. Hector knew two were enforcers, but he didn't recognize the other two.

More enforcers? Or were they trackers?

Hector didn't bother speculating. He would find out soon enough if Alpha Kontra wanted to know.

"I'm Alpha Alberto," the alpha proclaimed as soon as everyone had turned off their bikes. "Who's the leader here?" Then his focus spotted Hector, since he'd take off his helmet. "You! You were banished. Hector Ramirez, your life is forfeit for returning to my territory. Beta Grange, take him—"

Alpha Kontra cut him off as he swung off his *Harley*. Everyone else, including Hector and Ronnie, were following suit. "Actually, according to by-law Sixteen-C of the Shifter Accords, because Hector Ramirez is now part of my pack, I am well within my rights to bring him with me to any pack I deem necessary." He leaned against his motorcycle's seat with one booted foot crossed over the other. "I'm Alpha Kontra Belikov. I come under Shifter Council order Six-A to announce my presence in your territory for a short time."

"What nonsense is this?" one of the strangers snarled.

Alpha Alberto lifted a hand. Anyone with half a brain

75

would know that he was calling for the guy to zip it. The guy evidently didn't have a brain.

"Shifter Council guidelines?" he stated belligerently, crossing his arms and curling his lips in a sneer. "Who gives a flying fuck about some group of old shifter geezers?"

"Silence!" Alpha Alberto snapped.

The speaker scowled at Alpha Alberto, obviously not pleased at being scolded.

Alpha Alberto frowned as he stared intently at Kontra. "And why are you in my territory, Alpha Kontra?"

"To see Maria Ramirez." Alpha Kontra used a thumb to point Hector's way. "Hector's sister, of course. I understand they still chat."

Hector damn near felt the blood drain from his face.

Why did Alpha Kontra say that?

Saying that would paint a target on his sister's back.

"Do they now?" Alpha Alberto drawled. "How about that."

"Hector!"

Turning, Hector spotted Maria sprinting across the grounds . . . well, as much as a pregnant woman holding a baby and the hand of a toddler could sprint.

Holy shit! My baby sister!

Leaping forward, Hector moved toward her. He spotted the enforcers do the same. Fortunately, a few other members of the gang intercepted them, making certain Hector arrived first.

Hector wrapped his arms around Maria and clutched her tightly, leaving room for the babe between them. "Maria!" He threaded his fingers through his younger sister's hair. "Maria, are you okay?" Glancing at her swollen belly and the babe in her arms, Hector couldn't help but ask, "What happened?"

"Get away from her, faggot," one of the strangers who'd been standing beside the alpha bellowed. "Get away from my mate!"

Knowing his eyes widened, Hector murmured, "You met your fated mate?" He'd known his sister had been waiting, much to the displeasure of their parents, but she'd always had such a strong will. "When? How?"

"He's not my fated mate," Maria revealed. "I had no choice. I—"

"Hey!" The guy tried again. "Let me through, you bastards."

"If you don't release Enforcer Crespin, I will contact the council about you," Alpha Alberto declared.

A few of the men snorted and laughed.

Kontra glared at him. "Just try it." Then he turned to face Maria. "There is always a choice, Maria," he murmured in a soft voice Hector guessed he usually reserved for his mate. "If you don't want to stay with that man claiming you, you don't have to. You can join us." His gaze flickered over the tiny girl clinging to Maria's skirt, then the babe in her arms. "We'll take all of you." Kontra's gaze focused on Maria's wide, fear-filled brown eyes. "And anyone else who needs a safe haven."

Maria opened her mouth, then closed it again. She turned her attention to Hector. Her expression was clear—confusion and asking if Kontra could be trusted.

Hector smiled and nodded. "This is Ronnie Oleander." He pointed at his lover, who stood calmly by his side, silently lending support. "He's my fated mate. I met him in Wisconsin." Seeing the way Maria cocked her head, Hector shrugged. "It's a long story. Anyway, this is the gang he's part of, and they accepted us. All the guys are mated with other guys and . . . well, it would be a safe place for you and yours if you came with us."

"Yes, but you have to get Juan out, too," Maria whispered, glancing around uneasily. "No children should stay."

"Who is Juan, and how is he related to you?" Alpha Kontra asked, his tone gentle.

"He's my mate's half-brother," Maria admitted. "He's human, but Crespin brought him when he joined our roll." Again, she glanced her mate's way. "He doesn't belong here. He's twenty-two and should be able to live his life as he sees fit, and not be a slave to my mate."

"First, Crespin, is it?" Kontra questioned.

Maria nodded.

"He's no longer your mate." Kontra gripped Maria's shoulder. "As your new alpha, I sever his tie to you." His smile appeared kind as he added, "Your kids go with you, as you are obviously their caregiver. Hell, that little girl looks terrified of your sperm donor."

A slightly hysterical-sounding giggle erupted from Maria. "Sperm donor."

Kontra hummed. "Where is Juan?"

Pointing at a nearby house, Maria said, "In there. Probably cleaning something. Be gentle."

Nodding, Kontra pointed at the home in question. "Sam and Ryan. Gentle extraction of the human named Juan." As the men started forward, Kontra took the babe from Maria and deposited the infant into Noah's waiting arms. "Don't worry. He's raised a couple of little ones and knows how to care for them." Kontra then picked up the little girl. Hector found it interesting that she immediately put her head on the grizzly shifter's shoulder. "Go with them. Hector and Ronnie, you, too. Gather a few days' supplies for these youngsters. I'll go talk to your ex-alpha."

Hector obeyed, his mind reeling.

Maria kept shooting him questioning looks.

Ronnie finally murmured, "It's nice to meet you, Maria. Hector has told me many wonderful things about you."

That drew a genuine smile from her.

Fifteen minutes later, Hector gripped Ronnie's sides as he

drove away from his old armadillo roll. His sister sat behind Lamar with her baby cradled to her chest in a sling. The little one-year-old girl—Leticia—was cradled on Kontra's lap as he rode one-handed.

Juan appeared the most shell-shocked. The poor young human looked to be skin-and-bones. His brown eyes appeared sad and lost. Fortunately, he didn't have any trouble sitting behind Rueben on his *Harley.*

Hector mourned for the rest of his family, which he knew he would never see again, but he had a new family and a mate. That new family was giving Maria and those close to her a new start.

Nothing could be better than that.

Holding close to Ronnie, Hector realized his new life was just beginning.

YOU MAY ALSO ENJOY THE FOLLOWING FROM EXTASY BOOKS INC:

Backstroking with a Tiger
Charlie Richards

Excerpt

Tortelion swallowed the hunk of meat, enjoying the heady flavor of raw, bloody elk. Most humans probably assumed he was fed beef during a show, but the owners of the marine park went all out. Once Tort had realized he loved elk, they always provided it when he put on the show.

As a tiger shark shifter, Tort had spent over a hundred and fifty years living in the sea with the occasional visit to small seaside towns to indulge his human desires. The changes in technology made living like that extremely difficult, even more so for the owners of the park—brothers Kaiser and William Roush. They'd approached Tort and several other marine shifters with their idea to open a marine park.

Ten years later, the doors of World of Aquatica had opened on the coast of northern California. Years later, it was still packed nearly every day. The fact that the Roush brothers worked with a marketing genius by the name of Gracin certainly helped.

After Tort had eaten the last treat of the performance, once again soaking the first several rows of the audience, he swam slowly around the large show aquarium. He swam close to the exiting audience members, but not too close, so they could take pictures of his back and fin. Tort was always careful to keep any true identifying marks away from the crowd . . . not that most would ever notice the subtle differences between Tort and the other two tiger shark shifters that did the show — River and Caden.

Tort knew that twenty minutes after everyone exited the stadium, the gate to a series of corridors would open. He'd head through the tunnel and into a massive underwater aquarium. The rest of his six-hour shift would be spent swimming in there.

The loud splash of something hitting the water sent tingles across Tort's senses. Curious, he turned and swam toward the source of the noise. The thrashing of someone swimming in the pool piqued his curiosity.

Odd.

No other shifter ever swam in the tank during open hours.

The scent of blood teased his senses. Sweet iron-rich flavors flooded him. His mouth watered, but not with the same kind of hunger the blood of the elk caused. Instead, he felt something . . . else.

Desire, need, of a different sort surged through Tort. Confused and oddly aroused, he swam even closer. His sharp eyesight spotted four kicking legs, two bodies, and four arms. Blood dripped down the adult's scalp and dispersed into the water.

Just as Tort drew close, the adult grabbed the child and thrust him into someone's waiting hands. That caused the man to sink under the waves. He struggled, his limbs flailing, and bubbles erupted from his mouth.

More blood poured from the gash in the human's forehead. The guy's eyes appeared to roll into the back of his head. An instant later, the man's eyes closed, and he stilled.

The realization that the human had just passed out from

his head injury struck Tort just as another thought stabbed into his brain.

This human is my mate.

Acting on instinct, the need to care for his Fate-given other half of his soul, Tort dipped his head. He swam under the human and rose, catching the guy's torso across the front of his back and his fin. Ever-so-carefully, swimming slowly, Tort headed to the side of the tank where Gerard was crouching.

Tort fought his desire to shift and lift his mate from the water. Instead, he closed the distance between himself and Gerard. Resisting the urge to pause in the water, to make it easier for his fellow shifter to grab his mate—hell, sharks weren't supposed to be able to do that, after all—he kept swimming even as he passed Gerard.

Meeting his fellow shifter's eye, Tort spotted the worry in Gerard's gaze. Gerard heaved the human out of the pool and laid him out on the concrete ground. Tort circled, unable to help himself, needing to check that the human at least breathed.

Through the distortion of the water, Tort saw a shifter he recognized as Doctor Keller jogging toward the cluster of people around where Gerard had sprawled Tort's mate. There was also a small boy wrapped in a towel—probably the young human his mate had saved. A woman had an arm around the bundled-up youngster, as well as her second arm around a girl who could have been a teenager or thereabouts.

Water gods, please don't tell me my mate is married with kids.

Knowing he had to find out, Tort sank beneath the water's surface and swam to the far side of the aquarium. He rubbed his side against a tile that appeared like any other. It depressed ever-so-slightly.

In each aquarium and tank, there was a button. If for some reason a shifter had an emergency and needed to leave a shift early, the Roush brothers had even planned for that contingency, too. Each location had a panel that a shifter could push with their snout, body, or even a fin. It would set off an alarm in the security office, and immediate action would be taken to have the shifter removed from the aquarium.

Tort had never used it before. He hadn't ever thought he would, either. As a tiger shark, he was the toughest thing in his aquarium, and that was even if he hadn't been able to think and plan as a human. He didn't have any family, and as a shifter, he didn't really get sick.

The idea of running across his mate had certainly never crossed his mind.

It took everything in Tort to swim slowly around the aquarium as he waited. He saw Keller help his human turn onto his side and hack up water. Relief flooded Tort even as jealousy swamped him at seeing the doc's arm around the human's shoulders.

At least he's breathing.

Tort chanted that to himself over and over as he watched Gerard help Doctor Keller load his mate into a wheelchair and out of the area. Then Gerard ushered the remaining chattering guests out of the stadium. Seconds later, Eban and River entered. They closed the doors to the stadium-enclosed aquarium behind them.

Eban squatted by the water as River stripped down. "Cameras are off. What's up?" Eban asked, his brows furrowing. "If you just want to know about the human, Keller thinks he's going to be fine, but he's taking him back to his office to give him the once over just to be sure."

Willing his body to shift from shark to man, Tort felt his frame change. His tail split, his skin thinned and lightened, and his body and face contorted. Even under water, Tort could hear the crack of his bones, the creak of his tendons, and the pop of his ligaments as his human form took shape.

With a swish of his arms and a kick of his legs, Tort cleared the surface and sucked in a deep breath. He treaded water as he looked up at Eban. Blowing out a breath, he glanced between the other shifters.

"That human is my mate," Tort claimed without preamble. "I need to go to him."

Eban's brown eyes widened while River grinned.

"Well, damn," River responded with a grin. "Congrats, and get out of here."

Tort's fellow tiger shark shifter dove into the water and began to change.

Eban stuck his hand out, drawing Tort's attention. "I'll take you to him."

Tort grabbed Eban's hand and climbed out of the pool. He snagged River's cargo shorts and yanked them on. Next, he picked up the blue polo shirt and tugged it over his head.

Once Tort had slid on the discarded sandals, he fell into step beside Eban. The great white shark shifter was a security guard—what a standard shifter group would call an enforcer. Eban knocked his elbow into Tort's arm.

"Congrats, man."

Unable to stop his grin, Tort responded, "Thanks."

Now, if I can only figure out how to seduce the human.

ABOUT THE AUTHOR

Charlie started writing fantasy when she was eight, and after stumbling onto her first erotic romance at age nineteen, she realized her true calling. She now focuses on writing gay erotic romance, normally of the paranormal variety, with heroes of all kinds. With the help and support of her husband, Charlie finally fulfilled one of her life-long goals . . . move to acreage with her horses. You can often find her curled up with her laptop and a cup of tea or glass of wine, creating her next adventure. Charlie enjoys exploring the mountains of her new Oregon home on horseback, 4-wheeler, or motorcycle.

She can be reached at ch.richards2010@yahoo.com

Or visit her at www.charlie-richards.com